Praise for *Cupid, Inc.*

"WOW . . . This is an erotic romance that truly hits the mark. There are great, detailed scenes that leave you panting for more."
—The Romance Reader's Connection

"A top-notch quartet of tales that are guaranteed to singe your fingers. . . . What an enjoyable way to get revved up for Valentine's Day by spending it reading *Cupid, Inc.*"
—Romance Reviews Today

"I love Michele Bardsley's *Cupid, Inc.*! It's sexy and erotic, and the humor will make you grin at the same time you're squirming in your seat."
—Cheyenne McCray, author of *Forbidden Magic*

Other books by Michele Bardsley

I'M THE VAMPIRE, THAT'S WHY
CUPID, INC.

Upcoming releases

FANTASYLAND

continued . . .

Don't Talk Back to Your Vampire

Michele Bardsley

A SIGNET ECLIPSE BOOK

SIGNET ECLIPSE
Published by New American Library, a division of
Penguin Group (USA) Inc., 375 Hudson Street,
New York, New York 10014, USA
Penguin Group (Canada), 90 Eglinton Avenue East, Suite 700, Toronto,
Ontario M4P 2Y3, Canada (a division of Pearson Penguin Canada Inc.)
Penguin Books Ltd., 80 Strand, London WC2R 0RL, England
Penguin Ireland, 25 St. Stephen's Green, Dublin 2,
Ireland (a division of Penguin Books Ltd.)
Penguin Group (Australia), 250 Camberwell Road, Camberwell, Victoria 3124,
Australia (a division of Pearson Australia Group Pty. Ltd.)
Penguin Books India Pvt. Ltd., 11 Community Centre, Panchsheel Park,
New Delhi - 110 017, India
Penguin Group (NZ), 67 Apollo Drive, Rosedale, North Shore 0745,
Auckland, New Zealand (a division of Pearson New Zealand Ltd.)
Penguin Books (South Africa) (Pty.) Ltd., 24 Sturdee Avenue,
Rosebank, Johannesburg 2196, South Africa

Penguin Books Ltd., Registered Offices:
80 Strand, London WC2R 0RL, England

First published by Signet Eclipse, an imprint of New American Library,
a division of Penguin Group (USA) Inc.

First Printing, July 2007
10 9 8 7 6 5 4 3 2 1

For my daughter Katherine Anne
And for her Gigi

For my friend Evangeline Anderson
And for her mom

For my keeper Terri Lugo
And for her grandmother

*And so our mothers and grandmothers have,
more often than not anonymously, handed on
the creative spark, the seed of the flower
they themselves never hoped to see.*
—Alice Walker

ACKNOWLEDGMENTS

Kara Cesare totally freaking rocks! There isn't enough chocolate in the world to reward her for her patience, her sense of humor, and her enthusiasm. She is the editorial equivalent of an everlasting gobstopper.

Stephanie Kip Rostan is the best literary agent on the planet—and she's mine! Woo-hoo! When we first met, I had a Sally Field moment: You like me, you *really* like me! And she's never stopped—to my unceasing amazement. If I can't drive her insane, honey, *no one* can.

I adore Terri Lugo, who e-mailed me one day and said, "Can I help?" I hope she doesn't regret that I took her up on the offer. (Boy, did I!) Visit her at www.terrises.com.

I know that if I started naming members on my fan list who make me laugh and who boost

Acknowledgments

me up, I would run out of room or, worse, leave someone out. Just know, O loyal ones, that I adore you and will always be grateful for your wit, your charm, and your excellent taste in vampire fiction.

Gena Showalter is a *very* discerning reader. She e-mailed me about how much she liked *I'm the Vampire, That's Why*—and I didn't have to beg or bribe her, either! Take *that*, O cranky reviewers at Amazon! Hah! So go buy her books and visit her Web site and pay homage to her, all right? www.GenaShowalter.com.

All hail Google and Wikipedia! These online resources are the writer's best friends. I owe a debt of gratitude to irishgaelictranslation.com—an extremely helpful Web site with a terrific translation forum. And I couldn't live without (or at least I wouldn't enjoy life quite as much without) Dictionary.com.

As always, I express my eternal gratitude and love to Dean and to our children, whom I love to the marrow of my bones even when they annoy the crap out of me.

Foreword

Hi, there. It's me, Jessica Matthews O'Hallo-ran. I was the star (can you hear "Fame" blaring in the background?) of *I'm the Vampire, That's Why*. If you've picked up *Don't Talk Back to Your Vampire* without reading my story—shame on you! Oh, all right. Truth is, you don't have to read the first book to read the second book. Hell, I don't even get to tell this story—my friend Eva penned it (with help from our histo-rian, of course).

About three months ago, eleven of us single parents were killed by a slobbering beast. The

Consortium (or as I like to call 'em, Bossy Bloodsuckers) rolled into Broken Heart, Oklahoma, and turned us all into vampires. As if getting undead wasn't bad enough, we had to deal with a group of fanged assholes called Wraiths. Oh, yeah, the Consortium bought up everything in Broken Heart and is intent on creating a town for paranormal people. On the upside, I got hitched to a sexy vampire named Patrick. He has a sexy twin named Lorcan. *Lorcan and Eva sittin' in a tree . . .* snicker.

Don't worry, I'm still around. If you miss me too much, just go to our Web site: www.BrokenHeartOK.com.

Read on, people. Enjoy this book, damn you, or I'll sic the lycanthrope triplets on you. Do you really want to be a werewolf chew toy?

Didn't think so.

Yours in O Positive,
Jessica

P.S. I get questions all the time about a couple of things our historian didn't put in the book. Here are the answers.

1. What happened to Stan and Linda?

Foreword

Stan survived his injuries. Linda nursed him back to health, but though she dotes on him nonstop, she refuses to admit she has feelings for him. Stan not only admits his feelings, he talks about them nonstop to anyone who'll listen. But he's a human and Linda's a vamp. Linda refuses to Turn anybody ever, so they have a doomed relationship. There, aren't you happy you asked?

2. Why wasn't the binding sex scene between you and Patrick in the book?

Aren't you a pervert! Heh. Kiddin'. That was a very private (and hot, hot, *hot*) twelve hours. Patrick and I decided to keep that bit o' naughty to ourselves.

Chapter 1

When Lorcan O'Halloran, four-thousand-year-old vampire and professed Druid, fell at my feet, it wasn't to beg forgiveness for killing me three months ago.

Sunrise was imminent, but there I was on my front porch, teeth brushed, hair shining, wearing Happy Bunny jammies and matching socks, waiting not for a lovers' rendezvous or for the return of my teenage daughter, Tamara (she was listening to Marilyn Manson in her room... *shudder*).

I was waiting for a dog.

Well, he was more like a wolf. I'd befriended the poor creature almost a month ago—and I had fallen in love with the brute, whom I'd named Lucky. He hadn't come by tonight and I was worried. Ever since I got undead, animals *loved* me. They showed up at my house, hung out in my yard, and followed me everywhere. No one could account for this sudden odd attraction; I was starting to feel like a heroine in a Disney cartoon.

I was Broken Heart's librarian, a job my paternal grandmother had held until her death a year ago. We shared the same name— Evangeline Louise LeRoy—but that was our only link. My father died when I was two years old, and my mother had lost touch with the LeRoys long ago. Inheriting the job and the mansion/library had been a lucky break for me and Tamara. We needed a fresh start. I was ready for a different kind of life.

Admittedly, becoming a vampire wasn't what I'd had in mind. And neither was becoming an undead Dr. Doolittle.

Lucky usually loped in from the pocket of woods near my monster house, which was part residence and part Broken Heart library (think of it as a smaller, weirder version of the Winchester Mystery House). He always sat at the edge of my yard, watching me feed the other animals. I can't explain why I felt so connected to him, especially since so many other creatures vied for my attention. He always looked sad and lonely, and he never got close enough for me to pet him. It was almost like he wanted to be comforted, but didn't feel worthy enough.

What female can resist the lure of the tortured bad boy—two-legged or four-legged? He seemed scarred somehow. I wondered what had happened to him. Had he lost his mate? Most wolf species were loyal to their mates—serial monogamy, it was called—but not every sort of wolf mated for life. When I looked at Lucky, he just struck me as the type who was soul mate material.

I don't know why I looked up. Lucky had never arrived by air. Worry turned to confusion and then to horror when Lorcan fell out of the sky and rolled across my yard. I watched him struggle to stand and then weave toward the porch. While I stood rooted to the spot, he climbed the steps and reached for me.

I reared back and yelped.

Here was the man who'd killed me. He was the reason *I* was a vampire.

"Don't be afraid. Please." He swayed like a willow tree in a thunderstorm and collapsed at my feet.

Zarking fardwarks!

I crouched beside him and pushed away the silky black hair that covered his angelic face. He was beautiful—in the way that Satan was beautiful. You'd give him your soul and he'd eat it for breakfast. No, thanks. I'd already known that kind of devil.

"Lorcan?" I whispered. I felt monumentally tired. Sunrise was near. Either I took him inside or I left him on the porch. Since he was the brother-in-law of my friend Jessica, who had married Lorcan's twin brother a couple months ago, I probably shouldn't leave him to fry in the sun.

His eyes fluttered open, and that solemn gray gaze made me think of a lonely, scarred landscape. " 'On that bleak hill-top the earth was hard with a black frost, and the air made me shiver through every limb,' " I murmured.

"Wuthering Heights," he said hoarsely.

Then he smiled.

That smile went through me like a bolt of pure electricity. I was stunned by my response. Maybe it was because I had never seen Lorcan genuinely smile—his lips often curved in sad imitations, as if he were afraid to show real joy. Not that I'd ever had cause to get closer than ten feet to him, but still . . . my undead heart did a ferocious tap dance. I had never seen a man so heartbreakingly handsome. Other than his twin, of course. Patrick had a more ebullient spirit, especially since marrying Jessica. Lorcan, on the other hand, wore sorrow like a favorite coat. I had never seen him without it. Maybe he liked being penitent and grief-stricken.

Lorcan's hand warbled up like a bird with a broken wing. He cupped my cheek. "Evangeline LeRoy. Beautiful, you are."

The Irish brogue was thick, and hearing my full name uttered in that lyrical tone created another shock of electric lust.

"We need to get inside." I pulled him to his feet and he wrapped his arm around my neck.

The front door slammed shut behind us. To the left was a formal living room that I never used, except to get to the stairs that led to the second and third floors. The furniture was still draped with dustcovers. To the right was the double-door entrance to the library. In the middle was a long, narrow hallway. First door on the left led to my tiny office; second door was a private bathroom. Last door on the right—painted black, white skull and crossbones in its middle—was the entrance to my fifteen-year-old daughter's room: the lair of Tamara. Da. Da. Da. *Dum*.

As Lorcan and I walked past, the door swung open and my daughter popped out. Music blasted—a cacophony of screams and metallic bashing that made me flinch. "G'night, Mom." She gaped at us. "Holy shit!"

"Don't cuss," I said automatically. We both loved language, and swearing seemed such a waste of good wordage. However, Tamara had been cussing more and more often lately, probably to see how far she could take it before I did something disciplinelike. She was fifteen going on fifty. Despite her deep immersion in all things dark (and as the child of a vampire, could you blame her?), she was a sweet kid.

"Holy Zarquon's singing fish," intoned Tamara. She knew I loved the *Hitchhiker's Guide to the Galaxy* series. "Not quite as satisfying as yelling, 'Shit!' "

"Speak for yourself. I find 'zarking fardwarks' rather felicific."

"Wowser," she accused.

"I am *not* puritanical."

"You're not taking him into the basement, are you?"

"If you used your eyes, you could see that he's hurt and needs help."

Her gaze took in the six feet of hunk and she whistled. "His clothes are a mess, but did you see his abs? You could scrub clothes on that washboard. Yum!"

I rolled my eyes. "Can you control your hormones, please?" *I'm having a hard enough time with my own.*

Finally chastised, she hurried forward, getting ahead of us. I dragged Lorcan through the large kitchen and toward the thick metal door. The only safe place in my decrepit three-story house was the basement, where I had relocated after becoming, as my daughter put it, vampified.

The steel door was the Consortium's idea, as was the metallic glaze that coated the basement's walls—über-protection against light, which could kill a vampire. Not just the sun's rays, either; any bright, hot light would do.

Tamara opened the door. She patted my shoulder. "Sorry for being splenetic." She grimaced, obviously torn between being cool, indifferent teen and caring, worried daughter. "What should I do?"

"Just go to bed, baby. Everything will be fine by tonight."

She nodded. Lorcan and I hit the stairs, and the door clicked shut behind us. Even though it was pitch-black dark to human eyes, I could see just fine.

My sleeping quarters consisted of mountains of books, a huge yellow LoveSac—which looked like a giant's punctured tennis ball—and a king-sized cherrywood sleigh bed, complete with Tempur-Pedic mattress and extra-large, fluffy pillows. I was a pillow whore. There were six propped against the headboard. I was also a sheet snob: If it wasn't three-hundred-thread-count or higher, I wasn't sleeping on it.

The LoveSac was obscenely comfortable; I had napped in it many times. I thought about chucking Lorcan into it and throwing a blanket over him. Guiltily, I looked at the bed. It was the ultimate in sleeping accommodations, especially with its very soft sheets and plumped pillows.

"Eva," whispered Lorcan, "my chest hurts."

Guilt stabbed me anew. As gently as I could, I laid him on the bed. I flicked on the lamp that sat on the small bedside table. The pool of weak light wasn't much, but with my vampire sight I could almost see molecules in moonlight. Lorcan looked a mess, all right. His black pants were dirty and torn; his black dress shirt was in shreds. Blood streaked his chest, though the wounds were already healing. Dirt smudged his face, but in a boyish way.

I dug out a box of wet wipes from a paperback pileup on the floor and cleaned his face. Even though his shirt hung in tatters, I hesitated to take it off. Exhaustion poured heavily through me, and I knew I probably had only minutes before I passed out. Vampires really didn't have much choice about their sleeping habits—sunrise, you sleep, and sunset, you wake. No alarms needed.

"Your shirt," I said. "Can you—"

He muttered something in Gaelic, and to my utter shock the shirt disappeared. His bared chest with its dusting of dark hair was revealed in full. Tamara had been right—washboard abs. Yum.

"Jessica told me Patrick pulls that trick all the time," I said as I took wet wipes to the dirt and blood. I tried to sound blasé, but very few vampires had the power and talents of Patrick and

Lorcan O'Halloran. Making clothes disappear—and reappear—was rather impressive.

"I can do the pants, too," he said. His eyes flickered open and I saw amusement glitter in those silver orbs.

"No, no." I considered his jeans. "Unless you're hurt . . . somewhere."

"Oh, I do ache, love," he said in a liquid voice. His hand drifted to my hair and fluttered like a butterfly caught in a web. "I ache for you."

I knew then that he was delusional. If he wasn't out of his head, I might fall for those seductive words. It had been a really long time since I'd felt wanted, much less loved. Annoyed with the direction of my thoughts, I tucked Lorcan under the covers and grabbed a pillow. At least the LoveSac offered *some* comfort.

As I rose from the bed, Lorcan snagged my wrist. "We can both sleep here. I won't bite."

"Yeah, right."

I hadn't meant it as a reminder that he had a lethal bite. I couldn't snatch back the words now. Why pretend he hadn't killed me? Still, when his eyes went flat and he let go of my wrist, my stomach dropped to my toes.

"Forgive me, Eva."

The words were drenched in anguish. I felt as

though I'd held something pretty and fragile—
and it disintegrated because I'd gripped too
hard.

Feeling penitent myself, I brushed his long
black hair away from his face. "Rest now," I
said. "You can tell me what happened to you to-
morrow."

"*Damnú air!* Stop being so nice." He yanked
me onto the bed and I fell beside him. The struggle to get up and away from him ended in an instant.

Dawn was breaking—I didn't need to see it to
know it. I felt the heavy blanket of sleep draw
over me. But as the familiar darkness en-
croached on my consciousness . . . I felt Lorcan
drag me into his embrace.

Some vampires don't dream.

I don't remember dreaming, either. Not until
Lucky arrived. The first night he crept into my
yard, sitting dolefully at its edge and staring at
me with such sad longing, was also the first
night, or rather day, I dreamed.

It was the same dream every time—as vivid
and as colorful as a well-kept photograph. I
stood in a dark, thick forest, but in a little clearing where the tall trees cupped the night sky.

Looking up, I could see the round, pale moon and the single black-stoned tower that imprisoned something I wanted very badly.

I couldn't name this treasure. I didn't know *what* was in that tower. I just felt an incredibly sweet yearning . . . as if my life would be complete if I could reach that tower and take what was in it.

As usual, I wore a royal blue dress. It had wide sleeves, a square neck, an empire waist, and a straight skirt. My hair, which I never wore long, was piled onto my head, except for a few ringlets that draped my neck. On my feet were thin slippers the same color as my dress. I loved fairy tales, so it wasn't difficult to find a cause for my appearance—or for that matter, the dream's setting.

Just as I did every time, I plunged into the dank, creepy woods. Skeletal limbs pulled at my hair and tore at my dress. I pushed onward, desperation raking me with icy claws. I lost my shoes; my bare feet sank into the mud and were scored by sharp rocks.

Low growls echoed behind me and the chill of desperation turned into an arctic sensation of fear. Pushing through low branches and thick underbrush, I finally managed to reach the base of the tower. The growls grew louder, more menacing.

I hurried around the tower, searching for a way inside. There was no door, no hole in the stonework, *nothing.* In all the dreams before, I had never found the entrance.

But I did tonight.

I saw a sparkly gold rose appear on one of the black stones. Mesmerized, I pressed my palm against it. Stones disappeared and left a rectangle of black. The shadowy creatures chasing me burst out of the thorny brambles, so I dashed inside the magical door. It sealed up behind me instantly, leaving the monsters to scrabble and howl outside.

The tower was narrow. I stood before a twisting staircase. Blue sparkling orbs of light danced around the base. As my foot touched the first step, the orbs frolicked upward. Every time I advanced, they moved ahead, beckoning me. It seemed as though hours passed as I climbed and climbed and climbed. My bare feet chafed against the rough stones and my legs ached terribly.

Finally, I reached a doorway. There was no door, just an empty black space. Heart pounding, I hesitated. What I wanted so much was beyond the inky darkness. The playful lights bounced and twirled at the entrance, waiting for me to decide.

I stepped through. The blue circles raced ahead, bubbles of excitement, and lit the circular room. The only object in it was a huge four-poster. Silver curtains cascaded around it like a shimmery waterfall, concealing whatever slept behind.

I hadn't expected *this.* Frowning, I looked around the bed. What I was looking for was *in* the bed? Yes, what I wanted, what I needed, was there. Yet, I hesitated, afraid.

"Fear not, princess," whispered an other-worldly voice. "Would you give up now? When you are so close?"

Clutching the edge of the fabric, I drew the curtain back. Wetting my dry lips, I heaved a breath and looked.

"You found me," said the big black wolf. Then he leapt off the bed and tore out my throat.

Chapter 2

The prince longed to be loved by a maiden pure of heart and strong of spirit. He cared not for her upbringing or for her lineage. He wanted only that soul-to-soul connection, that true and honest knowing that love bound him to her and her to him.

For years he searched the world. He found beautiful women with quick minds and kind natures, but not one stirred his heart. Oh, he found pleasure. Nothing compared to the sweet moments held in a fair damsel's embrace, but those glorious touches never reached further than lips upon satin skin.

In his despair, he sought the advice of his grand-mother, a powerful witch.

"The one you seek has not yet been born," she said. "I can give you a potion that will give you immortality, but there is a price. You will never again walk in the light or sup at your father's table. To live, you must drink the blood of innocents. To find your maiden, you must embrace darkness."

"My soul will surely shrivel without the light," said the prince.

"Your soul mate is your light. Life is about balance. For every sacrifice, there is a reward." The witch stared at him, her rheumy gray eyes narrowed. "Beware, dearest prince! If you allow your new nature to overtake you, you will forget your quest. You will live only in darkness and you will never find the one destined for you."

—From *The Prince and the Maiden*,
an unpublished work by
Lorcan O'Halloran

Chapter 3

When I awoke, I found myself clutching Lorcan like a beloved teddy bear. He was awake, his fingers stroking my back. I scrambled to a sitting position and stared at him, embarrassed. With those silver eyes and his long black hair he reminded me of the wolf. My hand fluttered to my throat as anxiety prickled my skin.

"Bad dream?" he asked softly.

"Vampires don't dream," I said.

"You do." He looked at me, but his expression was unfathomable. "Thank you for helping me."

"No problem." *Big problem.* It seemed Lorcan's proximity affected me in unexpected ways. "What happened to you?"

"You need not concern yourself," he said, arrogance lacing his tone. " 'Tis done now."

What was done now? I didn't ask because I knew he wouldn't tell me. The O'Hallorans were good at keeping secrets. I watched him get off the bed. My gaze roved over the muscled torso. His chest was completely healed. Could I help it if my fingers wished to dance through those dark curls and flit across those ridges? I looked away and swallowed hard. When I looked back, Lorcan was dressed—a black T-shirt tucked into black jeans.

"Don't you like color?"

"Black is a color," he said. He smiled—the small, sad one he had perfected as the guilt-stricken vampire monk. I missed the other smile, the curve of lips filled with mischief. It was like glimpsing a slice of heaven before the gates shut. Hmph. I probably wouldn't see him smile like that again.

"Good-bye, Eva."

Startled at the sudden good-bye, I managed a limp wave. Strangely, I didn't want him to go. He made me uncomfortable and he confused me, but at the same time, I wanted to be near him. A red flag if ever there was one—as if my body didn't care what he would do to my heart. Lust had its own rewards. Yet mere pleasure glittered and faded, leaving only pain, only emptiness.

As Lorcan sparkled out of sight, he waved his hand and something gold and shiny fell onto the bed. I looked at the object and gasped. Picking it up, I fingered the full bloom of a gold rose. Real gold, too. The brooch was the size of a quarter. In the middle, very small, I saw a looped "L." For Lorcan? Huh. Was it a thank-you gift? Or a mark of possession?

I laughed. He probably made these little roses and tossed them at the feet of any female who showed him kindness. It wasn't special. Besides, vampires who wanted to put others under their protection—or as a step toward binding—had to put their claiming mark on the neck. It was magic; any paranormal creature would see a claimed being. I had claimed Tamara as soon as Jessica taught me how. She was my child, forever under my protection, and anyone who messed with her, messed with me.

Our symbol was a red ruby.

My mother's name was Ruby. She died five

years ago of cancer. Other than Tamara, my mother was the most important person in my life. Her death left a void in my world—one that had never been filled. I had learned to live with the hole. In fact, I guarded it fiercely.

The rose beckoned my attention again. It wasn't lost on me that a gold rose had opened the tower in my dream. Or that a wolf waited for me. I wasn't sure I wanted to think about that dream and try to figure out what it meant. Maybe it didn't mean anything.

I couldn't deny my attraction to Lorcan, but heaven help me, I *wanted* to deny it. I had a history of falling for men who were bad for me. Chances were good that if I was attracted to a man, he was shit in an expensive suit. Then again, Lorcan had already done the worst thing ever, hadn't he? *You are having sexual feelings for your murderer, Miss LeRoy? Tsk, tsk.*

Hard to believe it had been nearly three months since Lorcan noshed on my neck. If you've ever read those romance novels where the soul-tortured vampire hero reluctantly brings his mortal woman to the Other Side—well, my experience was the exact opposite of that.

I had just returned from an ice cream run

and had gotten out of my little VW bug. As I shut the door, I heard a shuffling noise behind me, followed by a hair-raising growl. There was *nothing* sexy about big furry paws grabbing my hips and sharp, icky teeth digging into my throat. The scariest thing about what happened was that I couldn't see my attacker. I *felt* him—he was huge, hairy, snarling. When he was finished, he tossed me in the driveway and loped away.

Then I died.

The worst part was that I never got to eat that pint of Ben & Jerry's Chunky Monkey.

If the Consortium—a sorta vampire Peace Corps—hadn't rolled into town and brought several vampire Masters willing to Turn us, none of us would be alive. Well, *undead*. Y'see, Lorcan had been suffering from the taint, a terrible disease that affected only vampires. Everyone was scrambling for a cure, including the Consortium. They'd managed to rid Lorcan of it, but whatever they'd done seemed to work only for him.

When I woke up after the attack, I was latched to the neck of a vampire named Mortimer. Yeah, I know—someone named *Mortie* saved my life. After Tamara got over the shock of my death and my vampification, she often crooned lines from "The Monster Mash" just to annoy me. As for Mortie, he'd returned to his wife in London and left my vampire lessons to the other Masters who'd decided to stick it out in Broken Heart.

After we got all the vampire stuff straightened out, the Consortium revealed it had been buying out residences and businesses in Broken Heart. It wanted to build the first-ever paranormal community in the United States. Over the summer, nearly all the human residents had moved out. The town was practically empty, its buildings under constant demolition and construction.

Turning into a vampire had rid me of cellulite, acne scars, and crow's-feet. Yet other things had been taken away, too—sunrise and road trips and ice cream (oh, the joy of a Ben & Jerry's pint!).

My mind drifted back to the dream. Why was I associating the wolf with Lorcan? Because I feared him? Because I wanted him, but I was *scared* to want him? Finding a bed in a tower—a phallic symbol for sure—seemed rife with sexual imagery.

Having sexual relations was a serious business for us vampires. If we fed *and* did the mattress mambo, we were linked to the person of our affection for the next century. Needless to say, most of us were real discriminating about our love lives. Hmm. Maybe my subconscious was just working out my sexual frustration with the only man who'd shared my bed in more than a year. Granted, he'd only held me, not tried anything naughty (was that a sliver of regret wedged in my relief?), but still . . . Lorcan was hot. Movie-star hot. The kind of hot a woman like me viewed at a distance, wanting and wanting but never in a million years actually getting.

Oh, what did it matter? I had no intention of binding with anyone ever. Falling in love for me was like unwrapping a mystery candy. I wanted chocolate, but I always got licorice.

Still, it was hard to forget those eyes, that wild hair, that muscled chest. Poor, poor sexually repressed me. I thought about all the blood and mud I had wiped off. Why had Lorcan been attacked? Fear ghosted along my spine. We had problems with a group of vampires called the Wraiths. They were a nasty bunch, but they'd been routed out of Broken Heart a couple months back. I shuddered to think they or their vamp/lycan abominations were running around the town again.

"Hey, Mom," Tamara called down. "Your breakfast is here."

"Share your pancakes with Charlie," I said.

If I couldn't indulge in real carbs, I could at least get the faint taste of syrup-drizzled pancakes in liquid form. Charlie was one of my two favorite donors. Donors were humans who were paid to be vampire meals—courtesy of the Consortium. Most vampires needed only a pint an evening to survive.

Charlie was a nice guy, though a little on the shy side. He was smart and loved books; we got along well because my most favorite thing in the world, other than my daughter, was reading.

I took a quick shower in the private bathroom (courtesy of the Consortium) and drew on a pair of black capris and a beaded white halter top, both new purchases thanks to a cyber-shopping trip. My friend Jessica and my daughter sat at the computer with me and helped me (read: chose for me) buy clothing I probably wouldn't have bought given my druthers.

A couple weeks ago, after assessing my favorite pair of gray sweats and baggy T-shirt, Jessica insisted that my "librarian frump look" had to go. The thing about Jessica was that she had a heart—and a mouth—as big as Texas. You never asked Jessica for her opinion unless you really wanted it.

My purchases arrived yesterday, and this was my first foray into my new look, which Tamara had termed "sexy mama." I wasn't quite sure if that was better than "librarian frump." But I didn't have a choice about my attire, since all of my old clothes had disappeared.

Last night, Jessica hauled me to Patsy's beauty parlor and Patsy gave my brown locks a sassy new cut and highlighted them with red and gold. I followed her directions for "sexy-messy" hair and to my delight, scrubbing gel into it made my new bob look all . . . well, sexy-messy. Linda, the manicurist, also gave me a pedicure and a manicure. My toenails and fingernails were a frosted pink color called Fairy Dance.

I put on gold hoop earrings and tucked my feet into a new pair of white high-heeled sandals. "You look fabulous, darling," I said to my reflection. Then I winked at myself. Oh, Lord, I was such a dork.

As I closed the lid to my jewelry box, I spied Lorcan's gold rose. I had tossed it into a little slot with no intention of wearing it. Then again . . . I pinned it to the left edge of the halter and instantly felt as though I'd done the right thing.

I hurried up the stairs and into the large kitchen. On the left side was a nook with built-in seats and a small round table. This was where Tamara, wearing a black kimono, was eating pancakes with Charlie. Charlie was in his late thirties, with a balding blond pate, a round face, and pale eyes—like watered-down whiskey. He favored rumpled khakis and plaid shirts, to hide his slight paunch, and he always wore loafers.

A forkful of pancake was headed toward his mouth when he turned to look at me. His eyes went wide behind his black-rimmed glasses and he poked himself in the cheek with the fork.

"Ow. Shit!" The silverware clattered to the plate. He grabbed a napkin, blushing furiously as he rubbed syrup off his jaw.

Tamara howled with laughter.

"Tamara," I said sternly, though it took a lot of willpower to still the bubble of laughter in my own throat. I rushed to the table and tried to help dab, but he shooed me away.

"I'm fine." Obviously nervous, he finished cleaning his face. Then he pushed his glasses up on his nose and looked at me sheepishly. "You look very nice."

"Thanks." Was I crazy or was Charlie giving me the once-over? No way. Charlie was like a comfortable pair of slippers or an old, warm robe. He made me feel cozy. I did not like the stare he was giving me now. Smiling weakly, I looked at Tamara. She shrugged and returned to her pancakes, but not before I saw the little smirk that flitted across her lips.

"Are you ready, Eva?" Charlie stood up. He knew I didn't like to feed in front of my daughter. It was one thing to be a vampire and another thing to do vampire-like things around your children.

We went into my office. The big, decrepit desk was filled with papers, files, and books. Books lined shelves around the room and were piled on the floor. Two big leather wingback chairs were parked in front of the desk, but one was filled with—you guessed it—books.

Charlie sat in the empty one and I looked at him blankly.

"Er, how am I supposed to get close enough?"

Charlie grinned and patted his leg. Okay. I was getting really weirded out. He had been my donor for the three months I had been a vampire, and this was the first time I'd gotten these kinds of vibes from him. Like *he* wanted to bite *me*. Still, maybe I was being too squeamish. Even though I had accepted that drinking blood was the only way to stay alive, it still wasn't an enjoyable part of my daily ritual. I was probably blowing everything out of proportion.

"Well, then . . . I guess we should . . . uh, proceed." I clapped my hands together and perched on his knee. He bumped me up, like a lascivious uncle playing horsey, and I fell into his lap.

"That's better," he said. "Drink up."

He bent his neck and though I didn't want to move, I was at too awkward an angle to put my fangs into his artery. Wiggling closer, I put my arms around him.

"Yeah," said Charlie faintly. "Oh . . . yeah."

"What?"

"N-nothing."

I was hungry, so I dismissed all the weirdness. My fangs descended and I sank them into his flesh. The blood flowing into my mouth tasted like nirvana. Maybe I didn't like starting or stopping, but imbibing blood was nearly orgasmic.

Then I felt something moving along my buttocks. Something hard. Something *growing*. Oh. My. God. I wrenched free of Charlie and looked at him in horror. "What are you doing?"

"You're so beautiful," he said, going all dopey-eyed. His hand reached toward my breast and I batted it away. He pressed his hard-on against my ass and bucked.

"Stop it!"

"No!" he cried. He grabbed me by the shoulders and stuck his tongue into my mouth. I nearly gagged.

"Hey, Mom," said Tamara from the doorway, "you got a visitor." I heard the sharp intake of her breath and then, "Holy freaking crap. What are you doing to him?"

I pulled away from Charlie's sloppy kiss and tried to scramble off him, but he held on to me desperately. With my vampire strength, I had the ability to hurt him, but I was trying to free

myself without breaking his arms. Then he released me, so suddenly that I fell onto the floor.

"What the bloody hell is going on?"

Shock rooted me to the spot as I looked
up, up, up into the stormy gaze of Lorcan
O'Halloran.

Chapter 4

I was shaken to the core. First by Charlie's strange behavior, which was so un-Charlie-like that it was as if someone else was wearing his skin, and second by Lorcan's sudden appearance. He was the last person I expected to see. What was he doing back already?

Charlie sat in the wingback and stared at me. His eyes had the glassy look of a puppet's. Worry gnawed at me. Something was wrong, but was it him . . . or was it me?

When Lorcan reached down to help me up, Charlie yelled, "Take your hands off her!"

He leapt up, his fist cocked. Startled, I said, "Charlie! Sit down!"

"Okay." He dropped into the chair.

Uh . . . what the hell?

Lorcan's hand on mine produced an electrical shock. At least for me. His face seemed carved from stone as he pulled me to my feet. No one who paid attention could confuse him with his twin, Patrick, who had a more ebullient spirit and who wasn't afraid of wearing more than one color. Lorcan *always* wore black, like he was constantly in mourning.

He let go of my hand and grimaced. "I am not constantly in mourning."

I blinked. I hadn't realized I said that out loud. I looked at Charlie. "I think you should go home," I said. "Go home and rest. Okay?"

"Anything you say, Eva. Anything at all." He stood up and marched out the door.

Lorcan, Tamara, and I watched him go down the hallway and out the front door. Chewing on my lower lip, I said, "He's never acted that way before."

"Once he reaches his home, he'll be fine," Lorcan said reassuringly.

"Mom, you have the ability to zombify people."

"That's not a cool power," I protested. "Bending the will of others is kinda lame."

"All vampires have the ability to glamour," said Lorcan, "but the Family Romanov's talents go far and above memory wipes and"—he glanced at Tamara, smiling—"zombifying people. Obviously your powers are strengthening very quickly." His gaze flicked over me. "You must learn how to control them."

"Are you going to teach her?" asked my daughter with acid sweetness. "Or do you want to skip the niceties and just kill her again?"

"Tamara!" I bopped her on the back of the skull.

"Hey! That's child abuse." She frowned over her shoulder at me, then stomped away. I think people in China heard the door to her room slam. Guilt wiggled through me. Okay. Maybe I shouldn't have bopped her.

"She has a right to be scared of me," said Lorcan. "And to be angry with me."

"You think so?"

My policy was to right my wrongs ASAP. You never knew how long you had with someone and I always wanted things to be squared away in case—well, just in case. So I hurried to Tamara's door and knocked.

"You're sorry," said Tamara as I opened the door. "I know." She shook her head. "I'm sorry, too." She sighed deeply, as if this admission had cost her all the energy she had left. She sank onto her bed and closed her eyes.

"I love you," I said.

"I love you, too. Now go away so I can mope."

Grinning, I shut her door. Then I walked past Lorcan and headed toward the sizable foyer. The library wouldn't be open for an hour, but I had another nightly task to perform.

Lorcan followed me into the foyer. I opened the closet and dug out various bags. He helped me drag them onto the front porch. When all the items were out, we sat on the rickety porch steps.

Like I said, ever since I became a vampire, the critters had been drawn to me like rain to Seattle. Squirrels, raccoons, deer, rats—all creatures great and small wanted to hang out with me. They followed me like I was Snow White or the Goose Girl. Sometimes I could hear their thoughts, which were more like pictures and emotions than actual logic with words.

Tamara and I had accumulated a number of cats, which went in and out of the house like they owned it. I verbally forbade all cats to go into the library, and strangely enough not a one had set a paw in it.

Broken Heart didn't really have dogs—most of them had left with the people. I think the fact that we had real werewolves roaming the forests and the streets kept their lesser brethren from venturing into town. But cats—shoot, they weren't afraid of anything, not even lycan-thropes.

As the end of August neared, summer still clutched Oklahoma in a lovers' embrace. The air felt humid and hot, even now, when the sun had been down for hours. A breeze offered some respite and brought with it the sweet scent of honeysuckle, a flower that bloomed nearly everywhere in town.

"Why are you here, Lorcan?" I offered an acorn to a squirrel. His tiny little paws accepted the treat and he sat on the step by my feet to nibble on it.

Lorcan didn't answer. Instead, he stared at the animals scampering around my front yard. Finally, he looked at me and asked, "Don't you think your daughter has a right to be angry with me? I did kill you, Evangeline. And because of me you're a vampire."

"Everyone is entitled to their feelings. But feelings aren't actions. Actions say more about you than any words you could ever speak." I offered some birdseed to a bluebird that landed on the stair railing. "But words have power, too."

"My actions were those of a murderer. What does that say about me?"

"I didn't realize you meant to kill us. Planning the deaths of eleven people—nope, that's not nice at all."

"You know that is not true." He sighed. "I will never be able to pay enough penance for what I did."

"How do you judge what's enough? By how you feel or by what others tell you?"

"I don't know."

I knew what it was like to pay for a bad mistake. Maybe that's why I softened toward Lorcan. I wasn't exactly afraid of him, maybe because deep down, I could feel his pain. Literally. I don't know why I knew that the heaviness in my stomach was really his turmoil. He'd said my powers were getting stronger. Lorcan truly was sorry—in fact, he seemed to be in a permanent pity party.

Lorcan's gaze captured mine, and I felt my nonexistent pulse stutter. Desire skittered through me, too. I put my hand on his arm. "You'll be okay," I said, echoing words that my mother said to me many times, "if you'll let yourself be okay."

"I would be okay," he said, his voice razor-soft, "if I knew that my actions could be forgiven."

"Shouldn't you start by forgiving yourself? That would probably pave the way for others."

"Maybe I should start by asking your forgiveness."

Forgiveness wasn't on my mind. Lust, pure and simple, zipped through me—as sudden and potent as a lightning strike. Lorcan's eyes captured mine and for an eternity I gazed at him. I wasn't sure if I was ready to make real what my imagination had created. Was I just horny? Or did I feel something special for Lorcan?

I lifted my hand off his arm and the spell between us broke. I glanced around the yard. Though I welcomed all creatures (like I had a choice), there was one that had not yet arrived to see me.

Lucky was missing again. I hadn't quite decided if he was a lycan or not. He never got close enough for me to pet him, but each time he visited he came a little closer. I couldn't feel much from him other than deep, aching pain. I didn't know if my mojo had drawn him here or not. Maybe he knew something about loss, like I did, and that bound us together.

"Who are you looking for?" asked Lorcan. "It seems as though every animal in northeastern Oklahoma is already here."

I shrugged. If Lucky wasn't a lycan, I didn't want him run off by the very possessive guardians of our town. And if he was, I didn't want his secret out. I felt protective of him.

I peeked at Lorcan and saw him smiling. The sensual curl of his mouth was like a punch to my stomach. He was beautiful. Beyond beautiful.

"Wow," I said, fanning myself, "is it hot out here, or what?"

"Hello, Eva. Lorcan."

I looked up to see Ralph walking up the cracked pavement that led to my house. Ralph was the only single dad among the parents Lorcan had accidentally killed. As the father of active twin toddlers, Ralph was kept busy. He had a full-time nanny and cook, thanks to the Consortium, but I rarely saw him around town. He usually brought his sons to the library every couple of weeks. And he always came to the

Turn-blood meetings and the shindigs hosted by the Consortium.

I noted that Ralph looked really good in his dress shirt, jeans, and leather loafers. He had short brown hair and kind blue eyes, and though he wasn't much taller than I was, I could tell by the fit of his clothes that he was definitely muscled.

Next to me I heard Lorcan make a low sound that reminded me of a growl. I glanced at him, but he seemed to be looking at the two deer nibbling on a patch of grass.

"The library's not open yet," I said. "Did you already read all the Margaret Wise Brown books to Stephen and Michael?"

"A million times," he said with a grin. "But they love them—especially *Good Night, Moon.* I'll end up owing late fees. But I didn't come for books, Eva. I came to ask . . ." He cleared his throat, his gaze on Lorcan.

Lorcan returned Ralph's pointed stare, his black eyebrows rising in challenge. I could almost feel the testosterone thickening the air around us. Ralph licked his lips, then drew back his shoulders. "I was wondering, Eva . . . would you like to go out?"

"Go out where?"

He flashed that cute grin again. "On a date. With me."

I felt flummoxed. I hadn't been on a date in forever. Suddenly nervous, and flattered, and given Lorcan's gray-eyed gaze on me, very uncomfortable, I opened my mouth to say . . .

"Wait a minute," I said. "Oh, no!"

The Eva LeRoy makeover suddenly made sense. New clothes, new hair, new look—all because Jessica had been setting me up. I'd bet dollars to donuts my own daughter was in on it, too.

"Did they put you up to this, Ralph? A pity date?" I put my head in my hands and groaned. "I'm sorry. I fell for it, too."

"Eva, no." He stood in front of me, his hands tucked into his front pockets. "I told Jessica that—that I wanted to ask you out, but didn't know how. It's been a long time since I wanted to date."

Uncomfortable was far, far from describing what I was feeling now. Lorcan had somehow gotten closer to me. His thigh pressed against mine and it was rock-hard and warm. Even though layers of clothing separated us, my treacherous mind remembered his dreamy half-naked form, in excruciating detail, and had I still breathed, I would've lost the ability.

"Eva, are you all right?" asked Ralph.

Lorcan's hand cupped the back of my neck. "You seem flushed, darlin'. Are you feeling well?"

Oh, please. Vampires didn't get sick (if one didn't count the taint). Heat stroked me. I felt as though fingers and lips touched my flesh all at once. *Impossible.* I could feel every stroke, every lick. My body shuddered under the sensual assault.

"Eva needs breakfast, is all," Lorcan lied smoothly. "Perhaps you can call her later?"

"Of course," said Ralph. "Promise you'll think about it, Eva? I swear that pity has nothing to do with my motives."

All I could do was nod.

"Good. See you guys later."

Ralph waved at me, then used his vamp speed to run as far and as fast as he could. Whew. I couldn't blame him. I was acting weirder than usual—and that was saying something.

Lorcan eased away from me, his gaze filled with concern. "Are you really okay, love?"

Frenzy couldn't describe the state of my body.

How could I feel this turned-on? But slowly the fires burning me inside out cooled. Within moments, I felt somewhat normal, if less than satisfied.

"I can't believe Jessica talked Ralph into asking me out."

"She didn't," said Lorcan. "It is as he said—he wanted to ask you out. Jessica merely helped things along."

"Oh." I fiddled with a bead on the edge of my halter top. "Ralph's nice."

Lorcan leaned close to me and I felt my undead heart giddyup. I could almost taste him, his mouth was so near mine. I pressed my hand against the butterflies fluttering in my belly. "Is nice what you want?" he asked.

No, it wasn't. I wanted ravenous, passionate, can't-live-without-you *need*. I scooted away from Lorcan. His presence overwhelmed me. I felt embraced and repelled by it. Confusion reigned, along with the aching desire he inspired—probably in all females within three feet of him. Would it be possible, I wondered, to explore the physical attraction between us? We couldn't have true intercourse, but there were lots of ways to make love—and I hadn't tried all that many.

"What are you thinking about, Eva?"

None of your business. "I'm still wondering why you're here. You never did answer my question."

"Maybe I want to ask you out, too."

I laughed, but the sound that came out was more like a terrified squeak. "You're joking."

"Yes," he said. His eyes were as hard as pearls. "I was joking." His gaze flicked to the gold rose on my top. He touched it, as though it were a real flower, then looked at me, a half smile crooking his mouth. "I'm glad you like it."

"It went with the outfit," I said lamely. "Matched my earrings."

"Yes," he murmured. "Of course."

The moment stretched taut between us. Then he sighed and pulled an envelope from his back pocket. The Consortium's fancy "C" was embossed on it. I opened it and pulled out the single sheet of paper.

After reading it, I looked at him. Anger burned a hole right through me. "You can't do this. I won't let you!"

Chapter 5

"We're not taking the library from you," said Lorcan. "We're simply moving it to the new building within the Consortium compound."

The compound, which had more security than a movie star's wedding, was still under construction on the former site of the Barley & Boob Barn. Most of it was done, though. The largest building was the Consortium headquarters. There were also facilities for scientific and technological development, housing for staff and for donors, security operations, and even a prison. It appeared that one of those Chiclet-white structures had been built for the new Broken Heart library.

I loved my little library. Not just the books upon books, old and new, crammed on the dusty wooden shelves, but the library itself. The LeRoy home had housed the library practically since Broken Heart was named a town. The LeRoys were one of the founding families. This library wasn't just a storehouse of knowledge and of entertainment; it was also a family legacy and a heritage to pass down to other generations. Funny how much of a claim I made on it, considering I hadn't known of its existence until a little more than a year ago.

I balled up the letter and tossed it at Lorcan. The paper bounced off his shoulder and onto the step. "*You're* overseeing it. The whole thing. What am I supposed to do?"

"You will still be a librarian," he said.

I didn't want to be a librarian. I wanted to be *the* librarian. Before I came to Broken Heart, I was a single mother who made ends meet by waitressing. When I took over my grand-mother's legacy, I got the one thing that had eluded me my whole life: respect. I had a position in the community, a real job with a real purpose, and I was someone my daughter could be proud of.

"Why didn't Jess tell me?" I asked.

"She found out tonight. She was . . . angry."

I was sure he'd understated her reaction. "Angry" was probably a poor adjective to describe it. Jessica had been the biggest advocate of keeping Broken Heart as intact as possible. Her family, the McCrees, had been one of the founders of our town right along with the LeRoys.

"Jessica is not on the board and not privy to the decisions that we must make," Lorcan continued. "The fact is, Eva, the Consortium owns Broken Heart. We have to remake it so that we can implement our plans for a parakind community. The Broken Heart library will be incorporated into the new, secure building."

Terrible sadness washed over me as I rose from the steps and walked into the yard. Automatically I looked for Lucky. I knew, somehow, that he wouldn't come tonight. A deer cantered over to me and butted my clenched fist. I loosed my hand to pat her and looked up at the falling-apart Victorian with its peeling paint and sagging wraparound porch. The old girl was past her prime. I hadn't been able to do much to rejuvenate her, either.

The Consortium had loads of material—books, scrolls, and God knew what else—in its own library. Lorcan was the author of many of those books, too. I'd never thought that my little piece of bibliophile heaven wouldn't be able to coexist with the Consortium's.

"You can choose any place you want in the compound," said Lorcan. "Or any house in town. Whatever you want—I'll make sure you get it."

"Wait a minute. You're taking my library *and* my house?"

Lorcan flinched, as if I had slapped him. He nodded, but his gaze skittered away from mine. "The house is on the perimeter of Broken Heart's border. It's a blind spot for us. We need this location to strengthen our security measures."

"You're going to tear down my house! It's been here for more than a hundred years. It was one of the first buildings erected in this town." The deer wandered away. I looked at the pocket of woods that curved like a wobbly crescent around the LeRoy home. "We shouldn't destroy the history that's already here. We should preserve it."

You would think a four-thousand-year-old vampire would know something about preservation of the past. Or maybe he'd seen so many things crumble into dust, he realized the futility of saving anything. I walked back to the battered and paint-chipped porch steps and sat down. Gazing at Lorcan, I said, "Why did you deliver the news?"

"I wanted you to hear it from me. I'll work with you in the new place—how it's set up, what programs to implement, and so forth."

Lorcan the librarian. He knew more about books—more about the world—than I ever could. Bet he knew the Dewey Decimal Classification system backward and forward. Hah. He probably knew Melvil Dewey, who had created the DDC in the 1870s.

"Yes, I knew him," said Lorcan.

I frowned. "Wait a minute. I didn't *say* anything about Melvil Dewey."

"Didn't you?" One eyebrow quirked. "Dewey was a brilliant scholar who loved the English language, despite always trying to simplify it. Bit of a lecher, though."

"He gave women employment opportunities," I said, defending the man.

Lorcan nodded. "True. But he was a man of his

times in many ways." He waved as if to dispense with the subject. "How long will you need to move out?"

Disbelief was like a splash of cold water. "You're serious." I stared at the squirrel near my shoe. He twitched his tail, his empty paws extended toward me. I dug through a nearby treat bag and gave him another acorn. "How long is the Consortium willing to give me?"

"As long as you need."

"Generous." The word dripped with sarcasm.

Lorcan said nothing. What else could he say? Shoot. I was used to loss. It should've been no big surprise to lose my job and my residence. After all, this old house and its crowded library made me happy. Happiness was fleeting. Hadn't I learned that time and time again? Comedian Denis Leary said happiness was a five-second orgasm or a chocolate chip cookie. How miserably true. I didn't care what Lorcan said about my involvement with the new library—it wouldn't be the same.

"I'm protesting," I said. "I'm going to appeal!"

"Eva." He sighed, and rose to his feet. "There is no appeal."

The finality in those words made me realize that fighting the Consortium's decision would be like pounding my fists against a brick wall. All I would get for my effort would be bloody fists.

"I am sorry," he said.

He opened his mouth as if to say something else—then apparently changed his mind. He stood there, silent, his eyes full of misery, and the tension stretched taut between us.

Finally, he sighed. "I suppose there is nothing more to say."

"There's always more to say," I pointed out. "The hard part is choosing which words you want to use."

His eyes glimmered with amusement, but the emotion was soon drowned by the ever-present sadness. "Until I find more appropriate words," he said softly, "I shall say good-bye."

"My mom used to say, 'It's never good-bye. It's until I see you again.'" I didn't know why I was trying to be so nice to a guy who had just delivered a bad-news bomb. All the same, I lifted my hand in a wave and said, "Until I see you again."

He inclined his head, his lips curving into an almost smile.

I watched in amazement as he rose into the air. He waved good-bye and zipped across the sky.

The squirrel finished the second acorn and

scurried onto my lap. No house. No library. No nothing. I scratched the squirrel's furry little head and sighed. He chittered, his brown eyes intent on mine. "Thanks, sweetie," I said. "But I don't think I can fit in your tree."

I looked around and not for the first time considered how far away my home was from town. The forest that curved behind the house marked the border of Broken Heart. Every so often I could hear patrols pass by as they made perimeter checks.

I suppose that from a security standpoint, the LeRoy homestead was very vulnerable. And that made us vulnerable. The idea that the Wraiths or something worse lurked just outside town made me shiver. I wanted the town protected, but more than that, I wanted Tamara protected.

Sometimes you get what you get. You can piss and moan, Eva, or you can look for the new opportunity.

My mother's philosophy had kept me on course for all my life. Even so . . . I looked at the decrepit building and wanted to cry, just a little. It was home.

But not for much longer.

* * *

Tamara, as usual, was dressed in unrelenting black. She eschewed the term "Goth," though she kohled her eyes, wore bloodred lipstick, and brought the word "sullen" to a whole new level of meaning. Her hair, which used to be the same color as mine, was cut chin length and colored raven black except for the two cherry red stripes on either side of her face. She also had both eyebrows and her belly button pierced with silver rings—and that was the *compromise*.

"Did you feed?" Tamara asked.

"Yes, Mo-*ther*." I finished tying my bootlaces, then stood up and stomped my feet on the old wooden porch. *Thud. Thud. Thud.* Sturdy. That was good, considering the terrain I was headed for. "Where's the flashlight?"

"In here," she said, handing me a black backpack. "So's your cell phone. I would've packed a snack, but y'know . . . *ew*."

When I was pregnant with Tamara, every kind of life cycle fascinated me (for obvious reasons). I studied the moon phases most fervently because I was *way* into symbolism and the whole "light in the darkness" thing appealed to me. That's why I knew that tonight's lunar phase was the "waning crescent." Lord-a-mercy, I knew all kinds of useless information. Ask me how much water a new toilet flushed and I could tell you it was one-point-six gallons. See? My brain was a compendium of weird facts.

"Sunrise is in *one* hour," said Tamara sternly, snapping me out of my thoughts.

"I know how to tell time."

"I wasn't sure," she said drolly, "since you don't have a watch."

"I have acute vampire senses, thank you very much." I slung the backpack over my shoulder and saluted my worried progeny.

"If your senses fail, then it's ustulation via dawn's early light." She grinned evilly. "You don't want to end up a grilled steak."

"Ustulation?" I stopped my useless warm-up and gaped at her. That little fiend! "Reminding your mother that she can be burned or seared isn't very nice."

She grinned. "Nyah nyah. I used the word of the day before you did."

Tamara and I had a daily contest. The "word of the day" was chosen from a list we kept pinned to the wall. Whoever used the word first got ten points, and any use of the word during the rest of the day received five points. At the end of the month, we tallied 'em up. If I had more, she did any heinous daylong chore I wanted. If she had more, I forked over fifty bucks and drove her to the nearest mall.

"Okay, okay. You get a ten-pointer."

"Sore loser." She had that look—the one that said she was trying to decide if she should show indifference or concern. Sighing deeply, she said, "It's a dog, Mom."

"I know. But I'm worried about him. He might be injured."

"Or he might be at someone else's house mooching their food."

I didn't think so. Lucky wasn't a moocher. I knew there was something wrong—otherwise he'd be around.

Tamara gave me a quick hug, which was thoroughly unlike her. Showing affection to the parental unit was strictly verboten. Since she was in a mood to accept a hug, I risked kissing her cheek. She said nothing, but grimaced in a manner that suggested acid had been applied to her skin.

Chuckling, I jogged down the steps to the cracked sidewalk meandering through the huge, weed-filled front yard. I waved to her, she waved back, then *vroom*—I was outta there. Tee-hee. Using my new powers to put on the speed always gave me a thrill.

Within seconds I reached the area me 'n Tamara had named Ooky Spooky Woods. Broken Heart was surrounded by pockets of thick, tangled brush and densely packed trees.

You'd think a vampire with the ability to run fast, jump high, and hit hard wouldn't be afraid of walking into a little ol' forest at four a.m. Still, my non-beating heart gave a little squeeze as I entered the woods. Leaves crunched and twigs snapped under my boots. I was tempted to get out the flashlight, but truthfully, I could see perfectly well.

"Lucky," I called. "Here, boy! C'mon, sweetie. Where are you?"

A gold-furred cat wearing an ankh around her neck leapt onto a fallen trunk and sauntered toward me. She stopped about half a foot away and stared at me.

"Hi, Lucifer."

The cat dipped her head as if acknowledging my greeting.

I sat on the log. Lucifer watched me for a moment, then started giving herself a bath.

Lucifer was the only known vampire cat in existence. Johnny Angelo, 1950s movie star and reluctant vampire, accidentally Turned her. Jessica told me that Johnny's first donor had been a very drunk man. The alcoholic blood affected Johnny and before he knew it, he'd awoken in a Dumpster with the vampire cat sleeping on his chest. He claimed he couldn't remember Turning the cat, but there she was, fanged and feline.

I had met Johnny a few times, but he wasn't exactly talkative. If you looked up "brooding" in the dictionary, his picture was probably next to the definition.

"Meow," said the cat.

Funny, I couldn't really get vibes off her. She didn't seem to think I was made of catnip, either, like most kitties I ran across. She meowed again and turned around as if to say, "You are no longer worthy of my attention." She trotted out into the darkness, her golden tail waving like a flag as she disappeared under some shrubs.

Grabbing the backpack, I held it in one hand as I leisurely strolled in the opposite direction. My thoughts turned to doomed love.

I had been a starry-eyed seventeen-year-old the summer Michael Hudsen noticed me. Typical story of a crush gone awry—so key up the violins and hand out the Kleenex. Title it *Shy Geek Meets Handsome Jock*. Michael had just graduated from our high school and broken up with his cheerleader girlfriend. I couldn't believe he remembered my name, much less that I liked the color blue. (I don't like it anymore. Green is my favorite color. Blue sucks.)

Michael spent two months seducing me with words, flowers, romantic gestures. The week before he was leaving for an out-of-state college, I gave him my virginity.

He gave me Tamara.

I didn't bother going back to high school. Instead I got a job, opened a savings account, and checked out every available library book about pregnancy and parenthood.

Branches crackled and leaves fluttered around me. What the heck? I looked up, fear tingling my spine. Even with vamp vision, I couldn't see anything—or anyone—above me. "Big squirrels," I muttered. "Or raccoons. Mutant ones."

The brush was too dense and the ground too pockmarked with holes to venture off the path. I leapt over a log, suddenly nervous. *Chill out, Eva. You're a big bad vamp, remember?*

Then I heard it. Something loped behind me, growling softly. Being in the creepy forest with growling creatures reminded me vividly of my dreams. *Don't panic.* Could be anything: wild dog, coyote, mutant raccoon. I dared a peek over my shoulder.

The creature was huge and fast, coming at me like a lion after an antelope. Good God! It smelled like it had taken a bath in the sewer. *Lorcan?* No. Impossible. He was cured.

Terror skittered through me, ravaging my ability to think. The creature howled—an unearthly cry that vibrated my bones. I swear to heaven, I felt its fetid breath on my neck, its claws scraping at my back. I looked over my shoulder again. The thing had gotten closer, but not near enough to grab me. I could see its eyes, glittering with malice and hunger.

My death was in that gaze.

I veered off the path and dared the gnarled and tangled foliage. Immediately, my foot connected with a fallen branch. I couldn't stop the tumble. I went down hard, skidding facefirst into a knotty bush. By the time I'd extracted myself and gotten to my feet, it was too late.

The monster had caught up to me.

And he'd brought friends.

Chapter 6

An unearthly howl reverberated through the woods, but the terrifying sound didn't come from the three lycans drooling and growling in front of me. No, the noise came from behind.

I nearly wet my pants.

In the blink of an eye, a four-legged beast leapt in front of me. He had fur as black as a starless night.

"Lucky!"

He barked acknowledgment. Growling fiercely,

he forced the three scary beasts backward until I had enough room to run.

So I did.

Big bad vamp, my patootie. I was scared witless. I didn't hear any fighting or scrabbling or yowling. I didn't want to look back, but I finally dared it. I didn't see anything but the dark, tree-filled path, which is probably why I smacked into a large oak.

Stunned, I landed ass-first in a pile of rotted leaves and dirt.

I jumped to my feet, but couldn't quite get my balance. The three beasts burst from the brush on my left and I whirled, hands out, as fear pumped through my undead heart.

Terror chilled me as I backed against the large oak. The press of the bark on my back scratched me, but comforted me as well. The tree was big and strong—and somehow that reminded me that I could be, too.

Lycanthropes. The security guards hired by the Consortium were lycanthropes, or lycans—known to humans as werewolves. True lycans looked more like very big wolves and usually loped around on four paws. Yet these monsters looked like stray canines and were very much two-legged. They looked starved and abused. They watched me with dark, hollow eyes. One stood ahead of the other two—and I guessed he was the leader. A long scar curved around his right eye. His snout twitched as he scented me, those awful eyes watching me hungrily. I'd seen enough Discovery Channel specials to recognize the alpha. He would kill me and feed first. The other two would dine on my leftovers.

My stomach quivered with nausea.

Images battered at me. Pain. Needles. Electric shock. Fire. Chains. Screaming. Blood. I shut the door, my mind reeling from the horror of those flashes. These poor souls had been vampires, but they barely remembered their pasts. Now they were beasts. They had been tortured, brainwashed—transformed into . . . lycans?

"Eva! What the bloody hell are you doing here?" asked a furious male voice.

I followed the pure sound of pissed-off Irish up . . . up . . . up into the branches of the oak.

Lorcan peered down at me. "What are you waiting for? Jump into the tree."

Oh, yeah. I could jump. I bent my knees and surged upward, my arms extended. Lorcan grabbed my wrists and swung me onto the same sturdy branch he crouched on.

We watched as the beasts surrounded the tree, growling as they contemplated their next move.

Lorcan's gaze captured mine and I felt my nonexistent pulse stutter.

The alpha was smarter than the other two. He jumped as if his legs were springs, grabbing the limb above Lorcan and kicking the surprised vampire in the face.

Lorcan flew out of the tree. He stopped just short of the ground, hovering. I had to take my gaze off him because the growling beast dropped beside me, his snarling, stinky body less than six inches from mine.

"Go away!" He looked as if I'd slapped him. I swear that he actually made a move to leave— before he was helped by the fist of Lorcan.

I watched as the mutant fell out of the tree. He twisted in midair and landed on his feet.

"We need to go," said Lorcan.

I looked up through the thick limbs. "What happens when we run out of branches?"

He looked at me, brows raised. "Who said anything about *climbing* up?"

In the next instant, he wrapped a steely arm around my waist and *whoosh*—up we went, all right—into the black sky. The lycans scrabbling at the tree below us howled in despair.

"Woo-hoo!" I held on to his neck and looked around, excited.

He kicked up the speed and we zipped across the forest in nothing flat. Before I knew it, we were hovering above my house. I felt giddy. I enjoyed being wrapped around Lorcan. He felt very muscular and heaven knew he was handsome. It had been a long, long, *long* time since I'd felt a man's arms around me. As we floated to the balcony outside my bedroom, he was smiling *that* smile, the one that made his silver eyes sparkle.

"Can you go even faster?" I asked.

"Yes," he said. "But you wouldn't appreciate bugs in your teeth."

I pressed my tongue against my teeth—just to check. "Good call."

Even though we had landed, I hadn't freed myself from Lorcan's embrace. He seemed to notice this about the same time I did. The light went right out of his eyes and his expression flattened. "Please, forgive me," he murmured.

He let go of me like I was aflame, then backed away until a good two feet separated us. I was offended by his need to create distance. For heaven's sake, *I* should be the one running away and screaming.

"What were you doing out in the forest?" he asked.

I figured the best defense was offense. "What were *you* doing there?"

He ignored my question and studied my boots. "Hiking? It's not like you need the exercise."

"Because I'm svelte and cute?"

"Because you're a vampire."

I stared at him, brows raised. "I have a book in the library called *Compliments and Flattery: A Guide for Social Morons.* You might want to check it out."

His lips quirked, but he stepped farther back, as if physical distance would also give him emotional distance. Sheesh. Would it kill him to relax a little? "Don't fall over the rail trying to get away from me," I said. "I showered, y'know. I spritzed with perfume, too."

"I'm aware of your scent." His words held a dangerous edge that sent my pulse skittering. Then he bared his fangs, his eyes going red for a split second. Startled, I felt my stomach dive to my toes. His gaze lingered on my neck, though I wasn't sure if he was thinking about my fragrance or my jugular. Then his eyes flicked to mine. "Sandalwood . . . lemongrass . . . vanilla." His nostrils flared. "There's something else."

"Ylang-ylang. I mix my own perfume. I'm still looking for the perfect Eva aroma." I laughed weakly, feeling uneasy.

"You smell . . . um, nice."

"It's no problem, Lorcan. I'll get the book for you right now."

He shook his head ruefully. "I know how to give a compliment, *a stóirín*."

The Irish accent that barely tinged his voice thickened with every word. Those lyrical sounds went right through me: *pling, pling, pling.* "Prove it," I challenged.

He crossed the space he'd put between us and tugged the band out of my ponytail. "The sun weeps because it can no longer caress your skin or warm your lips." He sifted his fingers through my hair. "I do not envy the sun, Eva. But I truly hate the moon, because its light touches you in all the ways I cannot."

I swallowed the knot in my throat as sensual awareness danced along every nerve. He leaned very, very close, his eyes ensnaring mine, and whispered, "How was that?"

"Um." I licked my lips. "Not bad."

His gaze dipped to my mouth and for an

almost pulse-pounding moment, I thought he might kiss me. Then he blinked and seemed to realize he was sharing my personal space. He backed up a few steps.

"Stay out of the forest, Eva. It's not safe." He frowned, his black brows dipping ominously. "You could've gotten hurt."

"That's kinda ironic coming from you." It was a low blow, but he'd put me off-kilter. It wasn't like me to verbally punch at people, and I felt bad the minute I said the words.

"I can never, ever pay enough penance for what I did," he said. "I'm sorry, Eva, a thousand times sorry."

"Lorcan . . ."

He shook his head, stalling my apology. He rose a few feet into the air and hovered. Aw, man. I loved the sensation of zipping through the air. I really regretted that he probably wouldn't take me up again. "Eva?"

"Yes?"

"You don't have to exercise."

"Because I'm a vampire?"

"No." A smile ghosted his lips. "Because you're svelte and cute."

He shot into the sky and flew away. I wished I was part of the Family Ruadan, which was the only vampire sect with flying abilities. Lorcan was part *sidhe*. As half fairy, he could fly and any vampire Turned by him or his children could fly, too.

Me-oh-my. Tingling from his compliment, I stared at the sky and wished for his return. So much regret between us . . . so much possibility.

I'd been killed, brought back as a vampire, and heck, I had the same problems, same feelings, same joys and sorrows as a human. My diet was different, and I worked at night, but really, how much had changed for me? Life was for living, not grieving. That's what my mother taught me. She also taught me that holding a grudge weighed down your own heart.

Jess kept trying to incorporate Lorcan into the Broken Heart community. Not many of us had helped her. Not even Lorcan. He felt too guilty about what he'd done to ever be part of Broken Heart. Plus, he was feeling a little too sorry for himself.

Jessica had shown me some of the books he'd written—in many cases by hand—and he'd sketched and painted, too. He was a wonderful writer, but just as serious with his words as with his countenance. Was he afraid to laugh? Was he afraid that if he smiled or chuckled, the Turn-bloods he'd accidentally made would lynch him?

Forgiving somebody for the wrongs they've done you was more difficult than trying to catch a ride on a moonbeam. But it was far more difficult to forgive yourself: I knew this from experience. How many times had I wondered about the kind of mother I was? The kind of life I was giving Tamara? When she was born, I was single, unwed, and barely out of high school.

Yeah, self-forgiveness was a real bitch.

My mother, who'd never remarried after Daddy died, made her living as a waitress. She got me a job at Ralph's Restaurant, a little mom-and-pop place off the old Route 66. Waiting tables and reading books and playing mommy—that's about all I did for the first ten years of Tamara's life. I couldn't afford day care, but Ralph made sure Mom and I had different shifts so one of us could be home with Tamara. Then Mom got sick—and, well, life went from tolerable to terrible in a split second.

My mother taught me as much about dying as she did about living. I think she would've gotten a big ol' kick out of being a vampire. I shook off the old memories. No use being a Sad Sally, as Mom would say. *Can't buy beans with an ounce of regret.* I smiled. That was Mom's way of saying I could look at the past all I wanted, but I couldn't change it.

Exhaustion poured through me, sudden and heavy. Sunrise was near. My body went kaput the second the sun hit the skyline. I opened the French doors and closed them behind me. My old bedroom looked bare and lonely. My stomach clenched when I realized that soon the house would be gone. Razed and forgotten, like so much else in this town.

I left and hurried down the stairs. In the hallway, I pounded on Tamara's door. The wall of music went down half a notch as Tamara adjusted the volume.

" 'Night, baby girl."

"G'night."

The sad, beautiful sounds of Evanescence entranced me. I thought about Lorcan. How haunted he was . . . how beautiful, too. Not to mention clever. He had avoided answering my question. What *had* he been doing in the woods? And why wasn't he surprised to find the lycans there?

Chapter 7

*H*elp. *I need help. Please, someone help me.
HELP ME!*

I woke up, shoving off the covers as I scrambled out of bed. If I'd still reacted like a human, sweat would've poured off my brow and my heart would've pounded furiously. Though I had no bodily reactions to prove it, I was seriously freaked out.

Foreboding lodged in my stomach like bad chili. Cramps radiated from my midsection as cold streaked through me. Dry-mouthed and scared, I tried to shake off my duress.

I needed some nosh to settle my stomach and my nerves.

I dressed in a pair of faded jeans, a purple T-shirt with LIBRARIANS DO IT BY THE BOOK scrolled in gold, and a pair of purple flip-flops. The gold rose found its way onto the purple T-shirt. Was I a sucker or what?

When I got upstairs, I used my vamp senses to check on my daughter: slow, even breathing and steady heartbeat. She had never been a "morning" person, so I often made myself scarce until she'd had breakfast and a shower.

I went to my desk to search for my Consortium-issued cell phone. Not in the charger. Crap. The backpack. I had dropped it during my run-in with the hungry lycans. I'd have to go back and find it, but I sure wasn't going back alone. I used the library's phone and dialed Jessica's number. It rang and rang and rang until the voice mail came on. I left a brief message. Jessica rarely carried her phone and even when she did, she forgot to turn it on or kept it on silent.

Who else could I call? Jess was the unofficial leader of the Broken Heart Turn-bloods *and* she was hitched to Patrick, who was vampire royalty. If he didn't have an answer, he'd know how to find one. I had never called Patrick directly. I liked the guy, but he was intimidating. I felt too much like a peon around him and the other Masters. I didn't have a high school degree. I'd traded that for Tamara. I was a voracious reader, though. I devoured everything from literary classics to romance novels to celebrity autobiographies. I loved to learn—I just didn't have any fancy paperwork to prove it.

Pacing through the dusty shelves of the first-floor library, I still felt unnerved, though I couldn't remember an actual dream. Only those frantic words instilled with pain reverberated in my mind. I hadn't ever had telepathy with humans, much less with animals. The vibes I got off most creatures were fuzzy images and simple emotions. I thought of the starved lycans romping around in the woods. Had I been dreaming of them and simply added words to those terrible images I'd glimpsed?

I was starting to feel really dumb and paranoid. Maybe the nightmare and my strange agitation were a delayed reaction to last night's adventure. After all, I'd almost been monster chow. Then I'd been rescued by Lorcan. I wondered if Lorcan had told Patrick about the beasts.

I wasn't in the administrative loop—as evidenced by the letter stating that my job and my home were no longer mine. Following on Lorcan's coattails in the Consortium library didn't appeal to me at all. I sighed. Okay, that was a lie. The idea of spending the evenings with Lorcan among books collected over centuries held mondo appeal.

For the Broken Heart library, I had tracked down every vampire book I could find. I had shelves and shelves of nonfiction titles that had grown dusty from disuse. I also had shelves and shelves of paranormal fiction by Charlaine Harris, MaryJanice Davidson, L. A. Banks, Sherrilyn Kenyon, Rosemary Laurey, J. C. Wilder, and many others. Those got checked out a lot. I couldn't keep *Undead and Unwed* on the shelves. It was a freaking hilarious book, too, written from the first-person perspective of a vampire queen named Betsy. I had ordered two more hardcovers because the request list was twenty names long.

I would miss being the librarian. I would miss owning my house and being in charge of the little library. As much as I wanted to hold on to it all, though, I knew the futility of trying to escape change, of trying to forestall what was meant to be. Argh! It felt like giving up, and I hated to give up.

Library hours were from ten p.m. to three a.m., which gave me time to visit Charlie or Alison and afterward to putter around the manse doing librarian-type stuff. Charlie and Alison were two of four donors who'd moved into Jessica's old house on Sanderson Street. The century-old Victorian held too many bad memories for Jess and her family, so after she bound with Patrick, they moved into the old Silverstone mansion on the outskirts of town. They had been fixing it up room by room.

The two-story colonial home was once owned by an oil baron named Jeremiah Silverstone. The house squatted on fifty acres of fenced land. The Silverstones were one of the five families, along with the McCrees and the LeRoys, who had founded Broken Heart in the Sooner days. Jeremiah was an only child who never married and never had kids. About fifty years ago, he disappeared. One day, lawyers showed up and announced that Jeremiah had donated the house to the town. Then they promptly emptied it of all valuable objects. The town had been too poor to do anything with the property, though both a bed-and-breakfast and a museum had been suggested. Despite valiant efforts by more than one eager Realtor, no one had ever bought it.

So Patrick traded in his bachelorhood and his custom RV for a big ol' house, a wife, and three kids. The only thing missing was a family dog. No matter how much her kids begged, Jessica had never caved in to their wheedling for a house pet. She would mutter, "Not after the Hamster Incident, damn it," and the subject would be dropped. However, Jessica's no-pet decree hadn't stopped Patrick from acquiring a white and gray pony subsequently named Glitter, which he gave to his stepdaughter Jenny, a nine-year-old with a tiara fetish.

I went out the front door and stood on the porch, pretending I could breathe in the sweet night air. I knew far, far too much about the town because I had no life and so I had time to collect information as an unofficial historian. Granted, my efforts had taken a strange turn, since I was now documenting the paranormal events, too.

Help me, please!

My hands clutched the porch railing so hard it cracked. Someone was projecting their thoughts into my mind. I looked down at the split wood and grimaced. Jessica had told me that she and Patrick could poke around in each other's heads. Usually, only bound vampires could communicate telepathically, though the ability wasn't always limited to mates.

How had someone tuned in to me? Was it a vampire in trouble? Or an animal? An animal who could articulate words in English? Ridiculous. *Says the vampire.* I was a mythical creature, but I couldn't fathom a talking animal. As Tamara would intone, "You are a *doofus giganticus.*"

I had no idea if the pleas were real or just me losing my mind. If someone had managed to psychically reach me, I had no idea where to find them. I licked my lips. I was really thirsty. At the mere thought of blood, my fangs popped out. I ran my tongue over the sharp incisors.

I leapt over the porch railing and landed lightly in the front yard. I looked around, but nothing seemed out of place. The animals were gathering: squirrels and birds, deer and raccoons, snakes and mice.

No! Get away!

The fear vibrating in the words, in the thoughts, was very real.

Where are you? I ventured mentally, feeling like an idiot.

I'm in the woods north of the cemetery. Please help me.

"Sorry, guys, I gotta go." The creatures paused and stared at me. Feeling guilty about the temporary abandonment, I held out my hands in supplication. "I'll be right back."

That seemed to satisfy them. I hurried into the street, then ran at warp vampire speed. The cemetery was nearly ten miles away, but I got there in no time flat. I stopped at the edge of the woods, hesitating. The unspoken rule was that this area was off-limits. Three months ago, the Wraiths, vampires who thought world domination was a fine idea, had caused some problems for us. The Consortium responded to the threats by blowing up the cavern the Wraiths had been hiding in and, along with it, most of the Wraiths.

I'm at the edge of the woods, I sent out. *How do I find you?*

Don't! Get away! Nooooo!

Pain swiped at me as terror filled my mind like a heavy black cloud. Like one of those stupid girls in a slasher flick, I plunged into the dank darkness. Within seconds, my acute hearing picked up familiar growls and the mewling cry of a hurt animal. I followed the noises until I found a tiny clearing.

Hanging from the limb of a large oak tree was a small wire cage. Inside it was a sleek golden cat—Lucifer. She cowered and hissed, her eyes wide with panic as she scrambled around trying to find purchase. I'd be fritzing too if a seven-foot-tall beast was playing "smash the piñata" with me.

I recognized the lycan as the alpha that had chased me the previous night. But who had captured the cat and put her in the cage? The creature jumped and swatted the cage again, causing it to whip back and forth.

Help me! Help me!

I stared at the cat. I was way out of my element. I darted away and ducked behind a tree. No cell phone, damn it. I'd rushed out to this location without telling anyone, not even Tamara.

Lorcan. He was the one who could really help me.

The lycan's frustrated roar made the cat cry louder.

Help me! Help me! Help me!

Hold on, sweetie, I projected.

Hurry! Hurry! Hurry!

I wondered if I could use the mind-meld thing with Lorcan. He'd been an animal of sorts once, right? Without any real hope of succeeding, I sent out the thought: *Lorcan? I wish you were here.*

"Didn't I tell you to stay out of the woods?"

"Aaaaaaaaaah!" I scrambled away. Crap, crap, oh crap! Not two inches from the spot I had occupied was Lorcan. He squatted next to the tree, looking at me with raised eyebrows. Gold sparkles faded from his body.

"Are you *insane*? You just appeared out of thin air! Holy God!" I gestured at him like a mad scientist berating his lab monster. "You scared me to death!"

"I didn't incur your death that way at all."

I gaped at him, then snapped, "You might not want to choose a career as a comedian." Obviously, he hadn't been joking, but heavens above, he didn't have to wallow in the morbid every hour of the day. Argh! I was furious that he—he—just *popped* next to me without warning. But I was also relieved that he had arrived to save the day. I climbed to my feet. "How the Sam Hill did you know where I was?"

If I'd hoped to receive confirmation that my mental calls had reached him, I was sorely disappointed.

"Why did you come here?" he asked, pointedly ignoring my question. His voice was as emotionless as his gaze.

Well, he wasn't the only one who didn't have to answer questions. Besides, what was I supposed to say? *Hey, I heard a cat's telepathic plea for help, but I'm not crazy or anything*. Instead, I pointed toward the clearing. "Save the little furball from becoming a lycan snack."

In the blink of an eye, Lorcan rose, zipped to me, and grabbed my arm. He looked down at me, his silver gaze gleaming with anger. "We will discuss your disobedience later."

"Disobedience!" I wasn't sure if what I felt was disbelief or anger. "What century do you think we're living in? You can't tell me what to do."

"Yes, I can. Stay here," he ordered. "Or *you* will be a lycan snack."

Chapter 8

I frowned at Lorcan. Was that statement meant to be protective or was it meant to be a threat? I didn't have a chance to ask for clarification, because he rose into the air and flew toward the clearing. The growls and screeches still echoed in the forest, which meant the beast hadn't gotten the cage down yet.

"Well," I huffed as I crept toward the ongoing melee, "*somebody* got out of the wrong side of the coffin today."

I ducked behind a clump of bushes and peeked over the tangle of leaves. The lycan's *parfum de sewer* attacked my nose in such a heinous way that I pinched my nostrils shut.

Lorcan alighted on the limb and drew up the chain holding the cat's cage. The lycan howled, leaping and swiping to no avail. The second that Lorcan opened the cage door, Lucifer lit out of it like her tail was on fire. She skittered up the tree to a high branch, then leapt to another tree. She repeated this pattern until she was long gone. If that wasn't just like a cat! Not even a "Well, so long and thanks for all the fish" as she left her rescuers in mortal jeopardy.

Lorcan yanked the chain off, then dropped the cage onto the lycan's big, furry head. The creature shrieked in pain as the cage bounced off and rolled onto the ground. It stomped on the cage, clutching its skull and yowling.

Feeling sorry for it, I dared a peek into its mind.

Once, he had been a vampire. I grabbed that much from his lumbering memories, but no name, no Family connection. And I got those same flashes—the pain, the blood, the chains—as I had with him and the other two last night. Who had locked him up? Tortured him? And let him go in Broken Heart?

Not sure what to do, I glanced up at Lorcan. If

I hadn't had super vamp hearing, I wouldn't have heard the words he whispered: *"Níl neart air. I must release you to Tír na Marbh."*

He sailed out of the tree and dropped to the ground. To my utter shock, a sword made of sparkling gold light appeared in his hands. Lorcan's eyes were filled with compassion and sorrow as he raised the blade.

"Lorcan!" I leapt from my spot and landed in front of the lycanthrope. I crossed my arms to block his blow and he cursed a Gaelic blue streak as his wrist smacked into mine. The blade tumbled from his grip. The minute it left his hand, it sparkled into nothingness.

"What the bloody hell are you doing? I nearly took your pretty head off!"

"Wait just a—" I blinked at him. "You think I'm pretty?"

His mouth dropped open. Then his lips thinned and his silver eyes went flat. "Leave it to a woman to find a compliment in the fiercest of words." He put his hands together and the sparkling gold light sword reappeared. "Get out of the way, Eva, and let me put the poor soul out of his misery."

"No." I whirled around, my heart pounding—from confronting the scary lycan or telling off vampire royalty, I didn't know. I kneeled in front of the hairy, smelly creature. "There, there. It's okay. What's your name?"

The lycan stared at me, a gleam of intelligence in his dark eyes. He pointed to his mouth and shook his head.

"You can't speak. Okay. Then think it."

Faustus.

"Faustus."

Images filtered from him: his struggle among dark-robed figures, taken into a shadowy room that smelled of antiseptic, forced onto a steel table and bound with thick chains. Syringes took out blood and others injected the substance that had turned him into the mutated lycan.

"He was turned into a hybrid against his will." I looked at Lorcan and flinched at the steely expression in his eyes.

The lycan's roar warned me. I whirled around in time to get swooped into his big, furry embrace. I yelled, "Let me go!"

The lycan released me instantly. Experimentally, I pointed at him and said, "Sit."

His big butt hit the ground. He looked up at me like he was a puppy instead of a murderous Bigfoot.

"Stay."

Lorcan grabbed my elbow and yanked me out of Faustus's grasp. "What the hell is going on? How do you know about him? How can you make him obey you?"

I tapped my temple.

"Glamouring does not usually include telepathy," he said.

"You've seen the nightly act, Lor. Animals love me. This might be crazy, but I think I can communicate with animals who can also take human form. Or who were human at some point."

Lorcan looked at me as though I'd plunged his glittering sword into his heart.

"Are you okay?" I asked.

"Of course." He shook off whatever was bothering him. As Lorcan studied the lycan, I thought about Lucifer. I'd heard her thoughts—they were very human. If my hypothesis was correct, then she had been a human at some point. And if *that* was true . . . who was she?

Then Lorcan touched my elbow and nodded toward Faustus. "I can't transport all three of us. Will he follow you?"

"I don't know." I looked at the lycan. "Where do you want to take him?"

"My brother's house. It's closer than the compound, and it has suitable . . . facilities."

I looked at Lorcan. "I won't let you hurt him."

"I figured that out after you threw yourself in front of my blade." His hand drifted to my hair. I felt his long fingers stroke my temple. "Beheading is one of the few ways to kill a vampire."

"I know."

"You are either brave or foolish."

"Probably both." I felt unnerved by Lorcan's gentleness. It was like being touched by velvet wrapped around a sword point—one slip of the velvet, and I'd be cut by the sword. I stepped away from him. How was I supposed to react to his touch, to the look in his eyes? I had no doubt he was still angry with me. I was angry with myself. I'd used up my allotment of dumb decisions in my lifetime; I shouldn't have tried to rescue Lucifer without help.

"I'm sorry," I said.

He blinked at me. "What?"

"Do you only recognize an apology when it comes from your own lips?" I smiled to soften the reprimand. "I endangered myself by coming out here alone. I'm grateful you showed up and prevented me from doing something really stupid." I swallowed hard, filled up by emotions I couldn't name. "Thank you."

He stared at me, his silver eyes mercurial. "You are welcome, *a stóirín*."

I looked at Faustus. *We're going to help you. Get up, okay?* The lycan got to his feet, then grasped my hand lightly with his large, furry one, as if he realized his strength might hurt me. Of course, he couldn't really hurt me—a vampire healed quickly of most injuries.

Expectant, we both turned to Lorcan.

"We'll walk," he said. He strode around us and we followed. Vamp vision allowed me to see him clearly and I must admit I admired his backside. My heart hitched as I thought about what Lorcan must look like without his clothes. Although I'd seen his yummy chest, I couldn't help but think about the rest of him. Then I felt so guilty about picturing a four-thousand-year-old monk naked that I redirected my thoughts to all the tasks that awaited me in the library. But then my eyes coasted down Lorcan's well-defined back and his . . . oh, my. Black really accentuated his—no, no. *Bad Eva.*

As we left the woods and headed across the cemetery, I asked Lorcan if I could use his cell phone. I called Tamara, but she didn't answer either her cell or the library's phone, so I figured she was in the shower or listening to her music at eardrum-busting levels. I left two voice mails and returned the slim electronic device to Lor.

"What the fuck is going on?" asked Jessica. She glanced around the living room, which was roughly the size of Manhattan, and blew out a breath. "Whew. She's not skulking around. Stupid Cussing Jar! Jen's made a mint off me this week."

"Luckily, you married a rich man," said Patrick.

He draped an arm around Jessica's shoulders. They looked so good together. I admit I had felt both joy and envy when Jessica and Patrick fell in love and married. I hadn't dated much and I could count on three fingers how many men I'd invited into my bed. I hadn't thought that I was missing all that much until I saw the kind of love that could be had by soul mates. I sighed. *Soul mates.* There was no other word to describe the bond shared by Jessica and Patrick.

"She can talk to animals—animals who have a human side," said Lorcan. He stood between the huge red sofa and the big walnut coffee table. I stood behind the monstrous furniture, next to Jessica and Patrick.

"You can mind-meld with animals? That is so freaking cool!" exclaimed Jess. "Would you tell Glitter to stop shitting by the fence?"

"I . . . uh, that's gross. Sorry, but I can't command animals."

"Well, hell. She does it on purpose, y'know. Never the same spot, but always by the fence, and I've ruined more than one pair of sneakers thanks to her."

"Jess," I said, "I can't discuss proper poop etiquette with a horse."

Bored with the conversation, Jessica stared at the man sitting on the couch, apparently content to watch the big-screen TV. "Hey, son of a monkey butt, why are you here again?"

Johnny turned his baby blues on his host. His lips hitched into a sexy grin. "TV."

"Captain Obvious," she muttered.

"*Mo chroi*," said Patrick in a very patient voice, "shall we turn to the business at hand?"

I felt the power of Patrick's stare on me. I squirmed, feeling as though I'd been sighted by twin silver laser beams. "His name is Faustus?"

"Yes," I said. "And I still think sticking him in

the laboratory was . . . was . . . a tramontane act."

"A *what's*-it?" asked Jessica.

"She thinks we were wrong to put him in the containment unit," clarified Lorcan.

"Oh." She looked at me, hands on her hips. "Hybrids don't have the ability for human speech. Stan said something about vocal cord corruption or . . . *what?*" She waved dismissively. "C'mon. It's our sweet little Evangeline, not Hitler. Sheesh."

"You might as well let me in on it," I said. "I met Faustus last night, too. Only he had two others with him. Did you capture them, too?"

Patrick studied me, looking like a math professor trying to figure out a troublesome equation. "When Lorcan contacted us, he failed to mention that you had been part of his reconnaissance."

"I wasn't. I was—" *Searching for a rogue wolf.* I smiled weakly. *Think before you speak, Eva. Words unspoken are easier to swallow.* Sage advice from my mother—I wished I'd remembered it five seconds earlier. Lor apparently wanted to keep me out of whatever was happening. I looked at him, hoping to figure out his motives. As usual, his expression was stoic. "Uh . . . er . . . Lor didn't mention our meeting in the woods?"

"Now it's a meeting," said Jess. She threw her hands up and joined Johnny on the couch. "I married a vampire. A rich, sexy vampire. Is my life easier? No. I'm ass-deep in lycans, my mother isn't speaking to me, my kids want a dog—hey, was that *CSI*? Go back. No, the other way. Damn it, Johnny, give me the remote."

He handed over the TV remote control.

Patrick touched my shoulder. "You're from the Family Romanov. You have the ability to glamour. Obviously your psychic powers are different now that you're a vampire. Rare is the Turn-blood who has your kind of abilities."

"You mean not everyone is a pet psychic?" I asked.

Jessica snickered.

"There is only one other vampire I know who has similar abilities," said Patrick.

"What's his name? Maybe we can compare notes."

"Koschei Romanov," said Lorcan. "The founder of your Family Romanov."

While I digested that bit of information, Lorcan turned to his brother. "I know what you're thinking. And I do not agree."

"She has a unique talent," Patrick countered. "And she may be able to help us. In fact, she is probably the only one who can."

"It's not fair to ask her."

"Oh, you are speaking for her? Are you claiming her as your *sonuachar*?"

Lorcan's mouth dropped open. Then he clenched his fists, his eyes molten silver with fury. *"Go hifreann leat."*

Patrick grinned. "If that's the case, *deartháir*, then you cannot speak for her."

"I have an idea," said Jessica as she popped up from the couch. "Why don't you stop talking about Eva like she's not here and ask her if she wants to help?" She rounded the couch and stood next to me. "Hey, feel free to tell 'em to go to hell. They have this really outdated idea of chivalry. It's cute sometimes, but mostly it's annoying."

Patrick's gaze stayed on his brother. *"Ná glac pioc comhairle gan comhairle ban."*

"Hmph! *Is minic a bhris béal duine a shrón."* Lorcan relaxed, his fists uncurling, but his eyes were still ablaze.

"What did they say?" I asked Jessica.

"I don't speak Gaelic, but I do speak Patrick. It's a good bet that he said something placating yet sarcastic. He's good at that. Mr. Patience sounded pissed—so I'm going with 'Fuck off.'" Jessica grinned at her husband and her brother-in-law. Then she looked at me, her eyes sparkling with amusement. She pointed toward the double doors that led to the living area. They were open, so we could see the large foyer, the massive staircase, and the single door—which looked like it opened into a bank vault—underneath the stairs. "Here's the deal. We decked out almost the entire basement in science stuff. Stan about had an orgasm when we finished construction. If Linda didn't bring him meals, he'd forget to eat. Anyway, the lycan is there. He has developed a bad attitude. I don't need to hear him say, 'I want to kill you' to get his meaning."

"The other two must have a hiding spot around here." Patrick rubbed a hand across his forehead as if warding off a headache, which was a human habit. Vampires didn't get headaches. "From the tests Stan has managed to do so far, we've confirmed he has the taint."

The Consortium had told everyone that the Wraith leader, Ron aka Ragnvaldr, had infused the blood from murdered lycanthropes into vampires suffering from the taint. Ron had discovered not the cure for the taint but a way to combine vampires with lycans. The effects had been unexpected and terrifying. The problem was that the creatures weren't always controllable.

In June, several of the mutants had attacked townspeople. Only one had survived, and only because Lorcan had Turned her. My undead heart squeezed at the thought that more of these hybrids were on the loose.

I looked at Lorcan and wondered how he'd been cured. He had been a big, hairy beast when he'd killed me. What had the Consortium done to rid Lor of the taint? *Infused him with lycan blood, that's what.*

"Why did it work for you?"

Lorcan didn't pretend that he didn't know what I was talking about. "I'm one of the oldest vampires in existence, so I had the ability and strength to withstand the process. I was drained of blood and I fasted for as long as I could. Then I was infused with special blood donated from live lycans."

"Special?" I asked, wondering which lycans had donated their blood for the experiment.

"Ever hear royalty and nobility called 'blue-bloods'? Well, royal lycans literally have different blood from common lycanthropes," said Jessica.

"Who donated the blood?" I asked, unable to quell the question.

Jessica looked at Patrick, who nodded consent.

"Damian, Darrius, and Drake are royals. They donated the blood to cure Lorcan and they're still donating blood for our attempts to create a cure for everyone.

"The Wraiths haven't figured out how Lor was cured—they just think they have. Stan's been experimenting with a formula using royal lycan blood to cure the taint, but it's a long way from working. Meanwhile, Ron the Dickhead gets a sick thrill outta turning tainted vampires into rampaging lycans."

"He does more than that," said Patrick, grimacing. "He's creating minions to do his dirty work."

"How can you tell a regular lycan from a hybrid?"

"A true lycanthrope is a shape-shifter. He turns into a four-legged wolf. He has the ability to shift whenever he chooses. A hybrid is two-legged and hairy, like Bigfoot. He doesn't shift because he wants to—the lycanthrope blood changes him. He can't change back."

God, it sounded awful. Ron was truly evil to take a vampire already dying from the taint and make him spend his last moments on earth as a monster.

"You can help us prevent more suffering," said Patrick. "If we can find the other lycans, we can track Ron. We need to shut down his experiments, not only for the sake of Broken Heart but for all parakind."

"You want me to psychically connect to homicidal werewolves?" Terror rippled up my spine. "I poked at their minds last night, but I didn't try to talk to them. Whoever mutated them didn't care about how much they suffered. It was a very painful process."

"That's unfortunate," said Patrick gently, "but not helpful. We need to know where they're hiding, how many more there are, and if the Wraiths are nearby."

"Tell her the rest." Lorcan moved around the couch until he stood next to his brother. "Tell her what's going to happen to the lycans."

"We can't reverse the process." Patrick grimaced. Jessica stepped into his embrace and he drew her against his chest. "Tainted vampires who are starved and then infused with dead lycan blood eventually go mad, either from the taint or from the further mutation of their bodies."

"If the taint doesn't destroy them," said Jessica, "then the lycan blood will."

I looked at Lorcan. "And that means . . ."

"We must kill them."

Chapter 9

"Oh, my God," I said. "You're going to kill Faustus?"

"We aren't saying that," protested Jessica, but she couldn't quite meet my eyes.

"Eva, will you help us?" asked Patrick.

I looked at Lorcan, though I hardly knew why. It wasn't like we were connected. He wasn't my friend, much less my mate—so why did it feel natural to want to confer with him about the decision?

"You must follow your conscience," he said.

"Who are you, Jiminy Cricket?" asked Jessica.

She rolled her eyes. "Eva, why don't you take a gander at the lab? If you get too freaked, we'll skip the Amazing Kreskin show."

By the time we got through all the security procedures and Stan's explanation of the laboratory experiments and systems, I was ready to gnaw on any available neck. I shouldn't have skipped breakfast. Hunger coupled with information overload was beginning to affect my mind and my body.

It took eye scans, fingerprints, and voice analysis of both Stan and Patrick to open the thick metal door that led to the prison ward. When it finally swung open, lights flickered on in the narrow hallway and I peeked inside.

Three large cells occupied either side. It was easy to see inside them; the front wall was floor-to-ceiling clear plastic. The remaining walls were bright white. Sticking out from the back partition was a long, thin white slab that I assumed was for sitting or sleeping. The whole place looked like something out of a science-fiction movie.

"If you're wondering how prisoners pee," said Jessica, "there's a little button that opens up a toilet. Same goes for food distribution. Oxygen is pumped in and recycled through these filter things Stan invented." She pointed to the cell on the right. "The plastic is half a foot thick and is resistant to everything—bullets, acid, claws, fists, fangs . . . you name it. But Stan used his freakish brain to incorporate sound. You can hear the prisoners and they can hear you."

I nodded, but I wasn't paying close attention. I could hear Stan's heart beating. Hell, my ears were so attuned to the one human in our midst, I swear I could hear the blood slogging through his veins. My fangs were trying to poke through, but I resisted.

The cells visible from my vantage point were empty, but if the noises coming from down the hall were any indication, at least one was occupied.

"I'll take her," said Lorcan. He placed his hand at the small of my back and, with no other choice, I allowed him to guide me down the narrow hallway.

The moment Faustus saw us, he went crazy. He smacked the clear plastic with fists and swiped it with claws. Spittle flew from his muzzle as he growled and screeched.

Stop it! I sent into his mind.

He stopped pounding on the barrier. His

huge furry chest heaved as he stared at me. I looked at the scar on his face and wondered when and how he'd gotten it.

Want out. He punched the wall. *Out! Out! Out!*

Calm down. You have food, shelter, and safety. Nobody will hurt you.

You lie. He moved away and paced. *Escaped Wraiths. Betrayers! Die my way. Mine!*

My heart clenched. He knew that his time was limited—that he would die one way or another. *Faustus . . .*

He turned suddenly and pressed his palms against the divider. His dark eyes burned into mine. My mind flickered—like someone turning on a television.

I saw a man standing in a field. He was not alone, but the background was fuzzy—as if Vaseline had been smeared across a camera lens. The man wore a silver helmet with a red horsehair crest; over a leather shirt, he wore silver armor. The garment ended in long strips, showing off the silver leg coverings strapped on from knee to ankle. His feet were encased in leather sandals. On one side, a dagger hung from his belt, and from the other hung a sword. In his hand he held a long stick.

"You were a Roman centurion," I said. "How did you end up a Wraith?"

His lips pulled back in a snarl. I held up my hands in supplication. This was an emotionally wounded creature—a man confined to animal form. Why he had turned from gentle giant to angry monster, I didn't know. Sympathy wound through my fear. He was a trapped soul and he was suffering due to another's desire to persecute. Then again, the Romans knew a thing or three about persecution. Maybe that was why Faustus was attracted to the Wraiths in the first place.

I kept my gaze on his. *Where are the others like you? How many are there? Where are the Wraiths?*

He shook his massive head. *Possible to save us?*

I glanced at Lorcan, who watched our exchange with an impassive expression. Nervous, I tried to decide what to do. Lie to get the information? Give him false hope in order to further our cause? I swallowed my sigh. I couldn't bring myself to add to his victimization.

We don't have a cure for the taint, Faustus. Even if we did, what's been done to you is irreversible.

He nodded, his palms sliding away from the plastic, and turned away.

Please, help us, I sent out desperately. *Tell us*

where the other lycans are—or at least where the Wraiths are located.

Faustus didn't answer. Instead he dropped to his knees, lifted his head, and howled. The sorrowful noise made my soul ache with misery. *I'm sorry, Faustus. I'm so sorry.*

"This sucks." Jessica crossed her arms and huffed. "What are we going to do now?"

"We take measures to protect the town," said Patrick. "And we find the hiding places of the lycans and the Wraiths."

"Patrols are already casing the town's perimeter," said Damian, the head of security, who had joined us in the laboratory. One of three triplet lycanthrope guardians, whom I knew now to be royals, he was tall, well muscled, and always wore black leather. He also scared the poo-dilly-poop out of me. I was grateful to know that he and his brothers were on the side of the Consortium.

I stood close to Lorcan, trying not to look at either Stan, who smelled like a four-course meal, or Damian, whose blood seemed rather appetizing, too. As far as I knew, lycanthropes were not donors. Vampires needed to imbibe human blood, though we could live off of animals if necessary. I wondered where shape-shifters fit into the mix.

"If the prisoner isn't going to be of use," said Damian, "then we should terminate him."

"No!" Everyone turned to stare at me. Shocked, I realized the protest had issued from *my* lips.

"I know it sounds like a shitty thing to do," said Jess. "But, honey, he can't be saved. It's the kindest action we can take."

I shook my head, feeling too unnerved to voice another protest.

Damian, who'd been leaning against the counter, straightened. He studied me for a moment. "It is unfortunate, *Liebling*, but necessary."

I knew that he was patronizing me. He thought me cute and nice, but not a threat. Damian was strong and he was smart, but he hadn't considered the idea that if I could read one lycan's thoughts I could read another's.

"You don't think it's unfortunate at all," I said quietly. "You look forward to seeing the unworthy half-breed destroyed."

Damian was a master at self-control, but not even he could prevent the flash of stunned surprise that crossed his face.

"He didn't volunteer for the Wraiths' mutation program," I said. "Perhaps you understand something about that."

"Stay out of my head," he said in a low voice. He stepped forward, fists clenched. A growl issued from his throat. I recoiled internally, but though it scared me, I held my ground.

"What are you doing, Damian?" asked Lorcan in a polite voice. He stepped forward, half shielding me. "Surely you're not threatening Eva."

"No," he ground out. "I need to check in with my teams." With a heated glance at me, he stalked out of the lab.

Jessica poked my shoulder. "What the hell did you see in that furball's mind?"

"Nothing." I knew Damian's secret, but I wouldn't reveal it—not even to Jessica.

I turned to Patrick. "Faustus served Rome as a centurion. Once he was a good man, and even now he's a proud one. If he must die, allow him to choose his death. He deserves that much."

"I will take your concerns and suggestions to the Consortium," he said. "But in the end, the decision is not mine to make."

Bureaucratic pass-the-buck bullshit. I hadn't expected Patrick to fall back on a company line. Admittedly, I had always found it strange that a group of vampires had created a corporate environment.

Lorcan took hold of my arm. "I will escort Eva home."

"Yeah," said Jessica, grinning widely. "You do that."

"Why did you not feed?" asked Lorcan.

"Kitty rescue. Faustus delivery. Mutant mind meld," I said, feeling light-headed and weird. If I hadn't known better, I would've thought I was tipsy. "It's been a busy morning—er, evening."

"To say the least."

Once we had exited the house, Lor let go of me. I regretted the loss of contact. No doubt about it. Lorcan O'Halloran was yum-yum-yummy. Regret wiggled through me. For just a moment, I wished I were alive and normal and on a date. *Dream on, Eva.*

We walked down the driveway, which was dark, wide, and nearly a mile long. I supposed that at some point it was considered more of a road than a drive, but since it led only to the Silverstone house it hardly mattered what one called it.

"Who are your regular donors?" he asked.

"Charlie and Alison. They live at Jess's old place."

"Then I will take you there." He paused. "Perhaps not Charlie. He seems to have developed a crush on you."

I glanced at him. "Why don't you offer a pint?"

"No one drinks from me," he said.

"You still have the taint?" My heart did a loop-de-loop.

He shook his head. "No. But we are still studying the effects of the blood exchange that saved me."

"How did you get the taint?" I asked. I was being too inquisitive. My usual stance was that people were entitled to their secrets and their sorrows. If someone wanted me to know something, they would tell me. However, I'd plucked a secret from Damian's thoughts and now I was asking for one from Lor.

"It's a long story," he said. "And I'm in no mood to tell it."

"You only have one mood," I muttered. "Morose."

"What did you say?"

"Um . . . er . . . huh?"

"Have you lost your bravery already, *a stóirín*?"

"My badge of courage fell off," I said and snickered. "Hey, can I use your phone again?"

"Where is yours?" he asked as he slipped the slim device from his pocket.

I slapped my forehead. "It was in the backpack I dropped in the forest last night."

"I'll find it for you," said Lorcan. "Promise me you'll stay out of the woods."

I tried not to make promises I couldn't keep, so I kept quiet. I took the phone and punched in Tamara's cell number. It rang and rang and rang, then flipped over to voice mail. Frowning, I left another message. I dialed the library phone. No one answered.

"I need to go home," I said. "Tamara still isn't picking up the phone and that's not like her. I have to check in on her."

Lorcan tucked the phone into his pocket, then gestured me forward. "Let's go. But as soon as you know she's okay, you must feed."

"Yes, mo-*ther*."

Lor wrapped his arms around my waist, pressing me into his chest. I felt no warmth, no reassuring beat of his heart—yet the heat of desire bloomed in my belly and warmed me right through. I twirled my hair and tucked it between us so that it wouldn't blow in Lor's face. It was girly of me to do it, but I rested my head on his shoulder. It might've been my imagination, but I thought Lor's arms tightened around me. As we took off, I felt a little jump in my stomach.

The air blew coolly against my face, the faint scent of honeysuckle teasing me as we passed over the razed high school grounds. Three months ago, the Wraiths had blown up the high school in the hope that they would off most of Broken Heart's citizens.

The night looked like black velvet with the occasional piercing of diamond stars. Coasting through the air in the arms of a handsome man struck me as romantic. I smiled and flexed my hands against Lor's back. For a monk who spent most of his time reading and writing, he was finely built.

"Eva," he murmured. I thought I heard laughter in his voice.

We arrived at the house far too quickly. As we had the evening before, we landed on the balcony that led to my former bedroom. Still feeling giddy, I reluctantly pried myself out of Lor's arms. "Thanks for the ride."

"My pleasure."

If I hadn't known better, I might have described the emotion glimmering in his eyes as desire. If Lor managed to forgive himself long enough to pursue a relationship with a woman, why would he choose me? Mom always said that you had to be wanted for yourself, faults and all. She told me she'd had that kind of love with Dad—that they balanced each other. "Between us," she'd often say with a soft laugh, "we made a whole person."

"I'll see you later," I said, turning away from Lor.

He grabbed my hand. "Wait."

Surprised, I faced him.

We stared at each other for a long moment. His eyes shifted from silver to dark gray, his pupils contracting. Then he blinked and all I saw in his soulful gaze was yearning.

He cupped my face, hesitant. We had no real breath, no dance of pulses, and no frantic thud of heartbeats. But desire existed all the same. I could keep the past between us. Yes, I could use it like a wedge to keep us apart.

Just like he was doing.

Instead, I closed the gap between our lips.

His mouth captured mine and I melted into

his embrace, quaking from his sudden and gentle conquering of my lips.

Our kisses were tentative. Butterfly wings. Soap bubbles. Angel feathers.

Then I dipped my tongue inside his mouth. He sucked on it, causing hot desire to roar through me. *Lust backdraft.*

He gathered me closer still, holding me tight as his tongue warred with mine. My hands delved into his loose hair and I tugged, desperate as one of those television housewives. I wanted more, so much more than this—I wanted Lorcan.

Then, like a candle flame doused by the wind, it was over.

"Evangeline." He sounded ragged and hoarse and regretful. Frowning, he cupped my face once more. "I regret nothing."

"Why are you in my head? Why can you—"

"Ssshh. We'll talk about it soon. I promise."

I accepted his evasion, but it made me nervous to know that he could read my thoughts . . . the same way I could read his.

"Let's go check on Tamara," he said.

"You don't have to babysit me. I'm not going to ditch feeding." I pressed a hand against my stomach. "I'm starving."

Smiling, he laced his fingers through mine and, unable to resist his chivalry (or bossiness, depending on how you looked at it), I led him through the bedroom. He held my hand down all the flights of stairs and by the time we hit the hallway, I was feeling moon-eyed and tingly.

The silence was as thick and strong as a brick wall. No music? No TV? No pings from the PSP? The hair rose on the back of my neck. Had she gone out? I doubted it. It wasn't like her to not pick up the phone if she planned to go somewhere. She was as protective of me as I was of her. I couldn't catch my breath. Then I realized I was trying to inhale oxygen—an unnecessary action for a vampire.

Now every hair on my body stood on end. *Something's wrong.* I wrenched my hand free of Lor's, but he grabbed my shoulder to stop me. Without making a sound, he glided down the hall and paused before my daughter's bedroom door. Despite the fact that not a single light pierced the black, I could see perfectly well.

Fear pounded through me as I followed. With my heart in my throat, I watched Lor open the door.

We looked inside.

The boy, who looked like an escapee from a

punk rock band, dropped Tamara's limp body onto her twin bed. He spun, raising his arms in an attack position. Two daggers shot into his hands. They were at least six inches long, sharp on both sides, and aimed at me.

Chapter 10

With a snarl, I shoved Lorcan aside and in a nanosecond I had the intruder pinned against the wall by his throat. Fury ripped through me and a red haze descended over my eyes. My fangs elongated and I barely resisted the urge to plunge them into his flesh. "What did you do to my daughter?"

"I didn't hurt her!" yelled the boy. "I am trying to help her!" His accent sounded Russian, but I didn't particularly care where he hailed from. He brought the knives to my stomach; the sharp tips pierced my T-shirt and grazed my skin. "Let me go!"

"You can't hurt *me*." I pressed my hand deeply into his neck and he gurgled, his eyes bulging. "But I can hurt *you*."

His hands fell away, but his gaze held more frustration than fear.

"Eva," said Lorcan in a low voice, "we need to find out why he's here and what he's doing. You must not kill him."

Kill him. Yes. That's what I should do. I looked at the skin visible between my hand and his T-shirt. I contemplated sinking my fangs into his flesh and dining on him. Hunger wound through my anger and suddenly I couldn't resist dipping closer to the boy. *Kill him . . .*

No, a stóirín. *If you harm him, you will never forgive yourself. Let him go.*

Aggrieved by my own behavior, I released the boy, who dropped to the ground and massaged his throat. His fancy knives disappeared into his sleeves again.

"Tamara," I said as I rushed to her side. I smoothed her hair away from her too pale face. She was still breathing, but her pulse seemed shallow and erratic. Oh, God. Oh, God. I wanted to cry, but vampires weren't allowed tears. My hands fluttered around her. What could I do? She was so pale. Helpless to do anything, I looked at Lor. His gaze was riveted on her, his lips pulled into a grimace.

I followed his line of sight. On her neck were two spots of blood. Rage reignited in an instant. I wheeled around. "You little bastard!"

Lorcan stepped between us, just as I rose and lurched for the boy again. He said, *"Solas."*

Green balls of light flickered into the room. They floated around as pretty as dancing fairies. Had I seen those lights before? A vague memory flickered, then was lost.

I reined in my temper for the second time. I glared at the young man wobbling to his feet. He had loose black hair, cut in jagged lengths around his face. His shirt was black, as was his leather jacket, which was riveted with silver studs and chains. His jeans were faded and ripped, tucked into black biker boots.

"She's only fifteen," I said.

"So am I," he retorted hoarsely.

"You're a vampire," I accused. "You could've turned fifteen six months ago or sixty years ago." I felt a momentary sense of pity. No matter when he'd been made a vampire, he hadn't had a chance to grow up fully.

"I am not a vampire," said the boy venomously. "I am a vampire *hunter*."

Shocked to my toes, which after the last couple of hours I wouldn't have thought possible, I sank down next to Tamara and stroked her hair. Sick with worry and fear, I focused on my daughter. What had happened to her? Had someone attacked her? Or had she offered herself as a vampire snack?

"You are a Roma warrior," said Lor.

"And you are a *muló*."

"No matter what you believe, I am not a ghost inhabiting a man's form. I own my soul." Lorcan kneeled next to me. His eyes were alight with empathy and concern. "I can transport her to the hospital, Eva."

I knew he meant he would be able to zap her there. Older vampires learned how to dissemble and reassemble their bodies in a way that was very *Star Trek*. Only the really old vamps could take themselves and someone else. I nodded, even though it killed me to be away from her for even a few minutes. "What about him?"

"You will accompany Eva," said Lorcan to the boy. "After we get medical attention for Tamara, you will tell us why you broke into Eva's home and tried to kidnap her daughter."

The boy crossed his arms. "You cannot glamour me, vampire. I am resistant to your powers."

"I am not trying to bend your will," said Lor. "I'm reminding you that the Roma have a peace treaty with the Consortium. You do not hunt our members."

His dark eyes flickered with anger. Then he nodded sharply. "I will do as you ask."

Lorcan scooped Tamara into his arms. He leaned down and kissed my cheek. "All will be well, Eva. I promise."

He and my daughter disappeared in a shower of gold sparkles. I turned toward the Roma hunter. "Do you have a name?" I asked.

"Durriken."

He pronounced it "DOO-reek-en." His accent wasn't Russian after all. I couldn't pinpoint it, and honestly, I didn't care. Weary, starved, and eager to get to the medical facility, which had been completed mere weeks ago, I pointed to the door. "Let's go."

"You say the girl is your daughter, but you are dead."

"I had her before I got *un*dead," I snapped. "And you'd do well to remember to address your elders with more respect."

Durriken flashed a grin, looking more like the

boy he was than the warrior he claimed to be. "You are a mother, no doubt."

We left the house and though it killed me not to run to the hospital and leave Durriken behind, I knew it wasn't wise. Instead, we got into my yellow VW. Had I been alone, I would've raced through the streets and made hairpin turns. Unfortunately, my passenger wouldn't survive a crash, so I only went twenty miles faster than the posted speed limits.

By the time we arrived at the hospital, Durriken was clutching the sides of his seat and looking green. I thought it a fine, if petty, revenge. The cuts on my stomach had already healed, but my T-shirt was done for.

The new hospital had been built on the same ground occupied by the old Broken Heart hospital. It had been one of the first buildings bulldozed. The new building was three stories, white as the frosting on a wedding cake, and filled with state-of-the-art equipment designed to help humans and parakind.

Durriken staggered from the car, then glared at me. "Next time I will walk."

"Suits me," I said.

We hurried to the front entrance. Lorcan waited for us in the small, well-appointed lobby.

"Dr. Merrick says Tamara is stable. Her room is on the third floor. I called Patrick and Jessica. They will be here soon."

"Thanks." We followed Lor into an elevator. I felt dizzy and my fangs refused to retract. My stomach roiled. As the elevator stopped, I felt as though the floor was falling away. I grasped the wall and tried to get my balance.

"You must feed," said Lor.

"I will," I said, licking my lips. All the moisture seemed to have left my mouth.

Seconds later, I stood over my daughter's hospital bed. Tamara looked like a porcelain doll tucked into a cotton-filled box. An IV was inserted into her left arm and a device on her forefinger hooked her up to a monitoring machine.

A blond woman stood nearby. The buttoned white lab coat covered most of her clothes, but I could see the legs of her black slacks and her thick-soled black shoes.

She smiled. "I'm Dr. Merrick. Tamara is stable, though still unconscious. We're putting fluids back into her system." She gestured to the IV.

"What happened to her? Did a vampire . . ." I trailed off, unable to finish the sentence.

"I'm afraid so, Mrs. LeRoy."

"It's 'Miss,'" I said automatically. I reached down and took Tamara's hand.

Lorcan wrapped his arm around my shoulders. He held me close and I leaned in, grateful for his comfort. I'd never had another person to lean on. For a while, I'd had my mother to help me and then I'd had Tamara. Suddenly, I realized how alone I'd been. I hadn't allowed anyone to get too close. I had kept mine and Tamara's relationship as the cornerstone of my life. Without her, I had no one.

"Given her paleness and her exhaustion, it's my opinion that whoever fed from her took more than was necessary. As you know, most vampires need only a pint daily to sustain them. And most have more than one donor, so that each donor has at least forty-eight hours of recovery between feedings."

Would Tamara have offered herself as a donor? Somehow I didn't think so. Tamara might've been a kid, but she wasn't stupid. She knew the dangers of being a donor just as she knew the dangers of being alone with vampires. I was the only one with whom she was truly safe.

"She needed her mother—and I just left her there." Guilt stabbed at me sharply and without mercy. *My sweet baby.* My eyes ached with the need for tears. Instead, I clutched her hand and offered silent apologies.

I turned to Durriken. "Why did you break into our house?"

His gaze flicked to Lor. "I hunt the one known as Nefertiti. My grandfather hunted her . . . then my father did . . . and now I do as well."

"You tracked her here?" asked Lorcan.

Durriken shook his head. "My father and I heard about the odd town in Oklahoma and the stories about her bonding with the actor Johnny Angelo. We were told Angelo was here and so his wife must be here, too."

"How has she escaped you for so many years?" I asked.

"She has not been seen since the night she bound with Johnny," said Durriken. "My grandfather tracked her to Los Angeles and was close to capturing her. Then she just . . . disappeared."

He turned to look at me. "I was scouting near your home and I smelled her."

"Smelled her?" I frowned.

"The Roma have very developed senses, which helps us find our prey," he explained. "Nefertiti's scent was imprinted on me when I joined the hunt. And I can smell a blood-full vampire at twenty paces." His gaze flickered over Tamara. "I went inside to find Nefertiti, but she was gone. So, I tended to her victim."

Guilt washed over me anew. I had been within a fang's inch of hurting him.

"Thank you," I said. "I'm sorry that I nearly . . . uh, wounded you."

"If you mess with a cub, you risk the wrath of the lioness. You have the heart of a warrior. This I respect." He nodded approvingly, and darn if I didn't feel vindicated. "I must report to my father. Do not worry, Lorcan, we will not leave the area."

"If you need a room . . ." I said uncertainly.

"We prefer to stay close to the land, but I thank you." He bowed to us and turned to leave.

"Wait," I said. "If you know Nefertiti is bound to Johnny, then you know that to kill her is to kill him."

Durriken shrugged. "We do not wish to harm an innocent. But Nefertiti is not a Consortium member and so we can hunt her. She is subject to the laws of the Roma and she must pay for her misdeeds."

"What did she do?" I asked.

"She is a war criminal," said Durriken. "During World War Two, she was part of a special unit that was instrumental in the capture, torture, and deaths of hundreds of Roma."

Oh, my God. Nausea crowded my throat. "Why would she and her unit target Roma?"

"Why else? They wanted to exterminate us."

He hadn't exactly answered my question. Why would Nefertiti want to kill Roma?

Durriken wasn't sticking around to answer more questions. He bowed again to us, then left, the hospital door swinging shut behind him.

Since Nefertiti had fed on Johnny and had sex with him, she bound them together for the next hundred years. Obviously she hadn't done so out of love.

"I thought bound vampires couldn't be apart for long," I mused, thinking about how Johnny had spent fifty years searching for his accidental bride.

"It depends on the vampires and the binding," Lor said. "The bond between Nefertiti and Johnny was purely sexual. Bindings that occur between vampires with strong emotional ties tend to have more strictures. Johnny can travel where he likes, feed normally, and live as any other *deamhan fola*. But he cannot mate—not until his binding is complete." His gaze pinned mine. "Eva, did you know Nefertiti was in

Broken Heart? Is that why you were in the forest last night?"

I stared at him, unaccountably hurt. "Why would you think that?"

He couldn't answer me, but inspiration hit me like a two-by-four.

"You knew she was here." I crossed my arms and glared at him. "Who attacked you? And why have *you* been skulking in the woods?"

He drew me away from Tamara. "About a month ago, we started getting reports about a woman appearing and disappearing near donor homes. From the description, we believed it might be Nefertiti, but she's never revealed herself before. We thought she'd gone to ground."

"Why would you think that?"

"She disappeared, but Johnny remained alive and healthy," said Lorcan, frowning. "The same lycans that chased you also attacked me."

If he was going to give a little, I figured I could, too. "I was there because I was looking for Lucky."

Lorcan's expression was skeptical.

"There's this wolf, okay? He started hanging around three or four weeks ago. Every night he visits me, but lately he's been missing. I was worried he was injured, but maybe he just moved on." Sadness hit me like a wave. It was so silly to feel bad about the wolf.

"You were looking for a wolf?" His eyebrows rose nearly to his hairline. "And you named him Lucky?"

"Yes. He seemed to need luck. He always seemed rather sorrowful." I sighed. "He never got close enough for me to pet him."

"You have such compassion, *a stóirín,*" he said softly. "Would you feel better if you could pet your Lucky?"

It was an odd question. But still, I nodded. I wanted to hug that wolf and let him know that someone on this earth cared about him.

My fangs had finally receded, but I knew that if I didn't eat soon, I might well faint. I glanced at Tamara. She was still asleep, but the machine monitoring her heart and breathing beeped reassuringly. Dr. Merrick waved to me as she discreetly exited the room. "I've only heard about Nefertiti from Jessica. Why would she feed off Tamara?"

"Because she couldn't feed off anyone else. We alerted the donors and tightened security."

"But you didn't tell Johnny."

"No. We didn't know about the Roma, either." He looked worried. "I've never known the hunters to be rash. If they are hunting her as a war criminal, then I believe she is one."

"Poor Johnny." Empathy welled. He hadn't chosen to be Turned or to be married to a vampire. Obviously, he'd joined the Consortium in an effort to do something productive with his eternal life. But Jess had also told me how badly he wanted to get his hands on Nefertiti—and not in a good way. "Lorcan—"

"What is it, *a stóirín*?"

His voice was so gentle, so understanding, I wanted to cry. Instead, I placed my hand on his arm and sought comfort in that small gesture. "I think . . . I think Nefertiti has been with Johnny all along."

"What do you mean?"

"I ventured into the forbidden zone tonight because I heard someone call for help." I pointed to my forehead. "Psychically. Lucifer called me to that spot. Maybe the Wraiths captured her and gave her to Faustus as a plaything."

"Wait a minute. You think that annoying feline is . . ."

I nodded. "Lucifer *is* Nefertiti."

"Aw, shit."

Jessica's voice was low but vehement. I

whirled around to see her, Patrick, and Johnny standing behind us. Johnny's hand was still on the door's edge, keeping it open, but it didn't take a psychic to guess his thoughts.

Snarling, Johnny jerked on the door, wrenching it off the hinges. Patrick caught it before it crashed to the floor, but no one could catch Johnny. In the blink of an eye, he hurled himself out of the room and disappeared down the corridor.

Chapter 11

Believing no sacrifice was too great to find his beloved soul mate, the prince drank the awful potion prepared by his witch-grandmother.

For a whole day and a whole night, he suffered terribly. At the end of the second day, all that made him human had been burned away, leaving only his memories . . . and his hopes.

That evening, he awoke as súmaire fola— *bloodsucker.*

Every day, he found shelter under the earth or in caves. Every night, he traveled the planet, searching for the soul mate promised him. He obtained suste-

*nance from innocents, taking only what he needed.
He heeded his grandmother's warning:* If you allow
your new nature to overtake you, you will forget
your quest. And both you and the one destined
for you will never find each other or true love.

*And so he guarded himself against greed, against
desperation, against anger.*

Years passed.

Decades.

Centuries.

*Great countries fell into ruin and were rebuilt.
Mortals he befriended grew old and died. Again and
again, the cycle of death and rebirth filled the endless
stretch of time.*

And still the prince did not find his beloved.

*After a thousand years of wandering, the prince
sought the table of a fortune-teller. At dusk, he entered her tent and bade her to look into his future.*

*"Please," he begged. "I have given up everything
to find the other half of my soul. I can think of nothing else but of her, the one I can love, the one who will
complete me."*

*Though the fortune-teller feared the súmaire fola,
she looked into her crystal ball and told him the truth.
"The one you seek has been born and raised on a
small farm. She is a lovely lass of marriageable age,
though she rejects all suitors."*

"Tell me more," demanded the prince. "Are you sure it is she?"

"I tell you what the crystal reveals. It does not lie." She looked again at the swirling colors inside the globe. "She is well loved by her parents and her sisters. She is kindhearted and never speaks in anger. Her patience is legend. Ah, one of her many gifts is that of song. When she sings, all weep at the sound of her voice. Yes, my prince, she is pure of heart and strong of spirit. She is all that you desire. But she is a poor, simple maiden—will you still have her?"

"I have amassed enough riches for a hundred lifetimes," said the prince. "I have waited a millennium just to see her face, to kiss her lips . . . to pledge my heart to her. Where is she?"

The fortune-teller shook her head. "The crystal ball does not reveal her location. But if you go west, you will find what you need to continue your journey."

"How will I know her?"

"Hair the color of a raven's wing. Lips as red as the rose. Skin as pale as morning cream and a gaze the soft brown of a doe."

His vigilance had been rewarded! Excited, the prince paid the woman handsomely. As he left the old and ragged tent, he walked west and thought about his maiden.

Finally . . . oh, finally . . . he would embrace his true love.

—From *The Prince and the Maiden,*
an unpublished work by
Lorcan O'Halloran

Chapter 12

Lorcan, Patrick, and Damian stood outside in the hallway and discussed carpentry and security. Dr. Merrick had checked on Tamara and pronounced her on the way to recovery.

I slid more ice chips into my daughter's mouth. As sorry as I was to know Johnny was loose in Broken Heart chasing Lucifer down, I was grateful that his temper tantrum had shaken Tamara out of unconsciousness.

"Mom," she said, staring at my mouth, "you're getting all fangy. Did you have breakfast yet?"

"I can take care of that," said Jessica.

I leaned down and kissed Tamara on the forehead. "I'll be right back. Eat more ice chips."

She rolled her eyes, but dutifully put another spoonful into her mouth.

Jessica led me into the empty hallway and offered her wrist. I held onto her arm and pressed the pulse point against my mouth. Other than that first drink from Mortie, I had never supped on another vampire. I didn't know if it was the fact that Jessica and Patrick noshed on each other or that she was from a different Family, but her blood tasted different—sweet even. After I was finished, I said, "I feel like I drank chocolate."

"Our donors eat a lot of Godivas," she said, grinning.

We returned to the room. Tamara's gaze was all over the vampire twins and Damian. Damian was kneeling and fingering the bent door hinge. Patrick was arguing with Lor in Gaelic, so I couldn't understand a word.

"Those dudes are hot," announced Tamara.

Both Lor and Patrick shut up and turned to stare at her. Damian looked up and grinned wolfishly. My daughter's face went bright red.

She drew the sheet over her head, muttering, "You can stake me now."

Laughing, I tugged the sheet down. "If you think they're cute, wait until you see the guy who rescued you. He looks like somebody peeled him off the pages of a manga book. His name is Durriken."

"Yeah, well . . . I guess I'll have to thank him," she said with a slight shrug. I knew my daughter—she was pretending disinterest, but she'd darn well anticipate meeting the guy. Although I wasn't sure that introducing her to a boy who probably knew seven hundred ways to kill was a good idea. Then again, who better to protect her?

"How do you know it's raining cats and dogs?" I asked Jessica.

Jessica blinked. "Um . . . I dunno."

"When you step in a poodle," Tamara answered. "How do you get a bull to stop charging?"

I snickered. "You take away his credit card. What did the cow say to the horse?"

"Hot damn! I know this one!" Jessica did a drumroll on the side of the bed. "He said . . . why the long face?"

We cracked up. Yes, it was silly to giggle over

such crappy jokes, but it had always been a sure-fire way to lighten our emotional loads. My mother had started the Bad Joke tradition when she lay dying in the hospital, her cancer too far along to cure.

Patrick joined us. He put his arm around Jessica and kissed the top of her head. They looked like someone had smacked 'em with a happy hammer. I couldn't help but wonder what it would be like to know that kind of love. Those two always looked . . . *aglow*, for lack of a better word.

"Why did Humpty Dumpty have a great fall?" asked Patrick, his silver eyes twinkling.

"Oh, do tell," said Jessica.

"To make up for a lousy summer."

We all groaned.

"And I thought *our* jokes were goofy," said Tamara. She smiled, though, and I knew she was mentally adding it to our List o' Lame Laughs. She glanced at me. "I must admit Patrick's joke tickled my risibles."

"Your what-ables?" asked Jess.

"Risibles," I repeated. "It means one's sense of humor or one's sense of the ridiculous." I grinned proudly. "Darn it! Another ten-pointer! How did you remember the word of the day?"

I explained to Jessica how Tamara and I kept a word-of-the-day list and the rules of our little game. Jessica looked at me speculatively. "You knew Faustus was a cent-a-thing just from the mind pic he sent you."

"He was a centurion, or *centurio*. They were professional officers in the Roman army that commanded between sixty and one hundred sixty men—known as a century."

"Or *centuria*," added Tamara. "Was he carrying a *vitus*?"

I nodded. "That's a short staff, or *vine stave*, that most *centurios* wielded. They mostly used them to discipline, whacking 'em across the backs of their men."

"You guys are freaking geniuses. How do you know all this stuff?" Jessica asked.

I suddenly realized that everyone in the room was not only listening but also looking intently at me. Heat rushed to my face, though I didn't think I had enough circulating blood to create a decent blush. I looked at the scuffed toes of my hiking boots. "I watch a lot of History Channel."

"And she reads everything," said Tamara. "She's *brilliant*." Her tone defied anyone in the room to disagree. Pride peeked through my embarrassment.

"Yeah, she is," said Jessica. "Damn straight."

"Eva?"

Lorcan stood next to me, his fingers grazing my elbow. I could see that he wanted to talk to me alone. I waved again to Tamara and followed Lorcan down the hall and into a private room.

"It's nearly eleven," he said. "I will go to the library and see to its opening."

"Oh my gosh," I exclaimed. "I forgot all about it!"

The library was mine for only a little while longer and here I was, slacking in my duties. But then again, *nothing* was more important than my daughter. Still, I felt guilty.

He stood very close to me, his gaze on mine. "You are so beautiful."

Warmth suffused my cheeks. I shook my head, but I didn't want to discount his compliment.

He drew me into his embrace. "I fear that I am not good enough for you. That you deserve someone better than me. Someone like Ralph."

Ralph? I hadn't thought about him since the night he tried to ask me out. He was a nice guy, but he wasn't Lorcan. *You'll know when you meet the right one, Eva, because your heart will recognize him.* Mom was right. My heart keened for Lorcan.

"So, I don't think I'm beautiful and you don't think you're worthy. I suppose we'll have to work on our self-esteem issues."

He laughed.

Emboldened, I wrapped my arms around his neck and kissed him.

His lips met mine and I could feel his uncertainty. I tried to kiss away his doubts. Maybe lust could burn off all but the essentials between us.

Too soon, he pulled away. I felt dizzy with want, with need. As Jessica might say, Lorcan offered me melt-your-bones passion. I had never known this kind of mind-numbing carnality. I was uncomfortably aware that my desire for Lorcan was intricately connected to more than just a need for sex.

"Worry not, love. I will take care of the library." Lorcan's lips curved into his half-sad smile and he smoothed my brow with his thumb. "Stay with Tamara for as long as you can. There are rooms in the basement—you can shelter in one until tomorrow night. I promise you that Tamara will be safe during the day."

I hated the thought of not being closer to her

while I slept. But I knew that my daughter would be cared for and protected.

He gave me one light kiss, a promise, I hoped.

"Thank you, Lorcan."

He rested his forehead against mine and whispered words I didn't understand. "For protection," he murmured. His eyes were like a gray mist, filled with secrets I desperately wanted to know. When had I stopped fearing him? It didn't matter. I was very aware of my new feelings for Lorcan and they all involved heat and light and motion.

"Good night, Eva."

"G'night." I felt all moon-eyed and tingly again as I watched him sparkle out of sight. Eventually I would be able to do the same, but it took a while for Turn-bloods to learn their powers.

Feeling both giddy and bereft, I returned to the hallway. I glanced at Damian, who leaned against the far wall, looking at me. I didn't sense anger in him; in fact, it was as if an invisible wall had been put around his thoughts.

The lycanthrope jerked his head toward the end of the hallway and raised his eyebrows. I followed him until we reached the exit door. Once again, he leaned against the wall and looked at the floor, apparently gathering his thoughts. "Whatever you saw when you were poking around in my head . . . you must not believe first appearances."

For once, I could see past his tough exterior. I didn't think Damian the type of man who tried to correct another's impression of him. Why should my opinion matter? I didn't know, but all the same, I was flattered—and confused. I risked putting my hand on his arm. "I didn't poke around. I heard your thoughts and the image came unbidden. I have to wonder why you were thinking of it when you were also thinking of Faustus."

"I don't have to explain myself," he said stiffly.

"No, you don't."

He stared at me for a long moment. "Faustus reminded me of old sorrows. You see, the lycanthropes are dying out. We don't have many females and more than half of our pups born don't live past a year."

"I'm so sorry, Damian." Empathy welled. I was a mother. The very idea of losing Tamara terrified me. I couldn't imagine being a mother who knew that the child I bore had a fifty percent chance of dying.

He inclined his head. Sighing, he continued, "We are not unknown to the humans, especially in Germany. The Deutsches Reich knew about us. During World War Two, they raided our villages and took us to the death camps. Adolf Hitler wanted to build a master race, but he was thinking more along the lines of strength, near-immortality, and the ability to change form. But lycan DNA does not combine well with other species' DNA."

"Is that why the tainted vampires who are given lycan blood turn into those creatures?"

"The Wraiths keep using blood taken from lycans they've murdered. Such blood is less potent and more unstable. It changes them before it kills them."

The lycan-blood transfusion had transformed Lorcan. But he'd been infused with royal plasma from living donors. Obviously his body had a battle with the lycan DNA and he temporarily became the same kind of creature as the others. But Lorcan not only survived the process, he was cured of the taint.

"Thanks to the Reich, our small numbers got smaller. The women—they suffered the most." He paused, waving a hand as if he could wipe away such a terrible history. "They took our only sister—Danielle. She was the youngest of us, and as a girl, very prized, very beloved. We tracked her to a death camp. My brothers and I captured the guards and took their uniforms. The image you saw, *ja*?" He tapped his temple.

I nodded.

"We were too late to save her. We were too late to save anyone."

I didn't have any words for Damian. How could you soothe such a festering wound? I hadn't considered how human events and history had affected paranormal beings. And surely there was a whole parakind history filled with amazing experiences that no human had ever known about.

"Why are you telling me this?" I asked. "I sympathize, Damian. I'm truly sorry for your loss. But how can I help?"

"The others, they debate about you and your special ability. They think about how to use you to further the Consortium goals. And I—I think the same thing, Eva. About how to use you to serve *my* purpose."

I tried not to shiver at his intensity or show evidence of my sudden fear. "What do you want from me?"

"Nefertiti."

"Her dance card is getting full," I said, grimacing. The woman sure knew how to make enemies.

"You said she has been hiding in the form of Lucifer," said Damian.

I hadn't quite figured out *how* Nefertiti could turn into a cat, but I felt sure she was doing so. "My telepathy only works with animals who can take human form, so it's a logical conclusion."

"You are very smart, so I believe your conclusion." He nodded sharply. "I want her captured, Eva. I want her to pay."

I was still reeling from being called smart by someone who was, for all intents and purposes, a more advanced being. Then the words Damian had spoken filtered through my scattered thoughts. "Wait a minute. You want Nefertiti to pay for what?"

"For murdering my sister. Who do you think led the squad that captured her?" He laughed bitterly. "I'll give you one guess who instigated the hunts and who made a deal with the Reich."

"Ron, the esteemed leader of the Wraiths."

He nodded sharply. Another kind of grief was filtering out from his psychic protections. I couldn't argue that he mourned his sister's death, but there was a deeper reason for his need for vengeance.

"Why not let the Roma track and capture her?"

"Nein und abermals nein!"

Surprised at his vehemence, I took a step back. He made a visible effort to control his temper.

"What's your problem with the Roma?"

"In a way, the lycanthropes and the Roma are cousins, if you will. Our legacy is to protect vampires and theirs is to hunt them."

"You mean Durriken and other Roma can turn into werewolves?"

"Only one night each month—on the full moon."

"And you don't mate with them because . . ."

His face went white, not with fury, but with pain. There was a story, I was sure. I was a hair shy of delving into his thoughts to assuage my curiosity, but I didn't.

"We will not mate with Roma. It is a royal decree."

The words sounded as if they'd been pulled out by force. To change the subject, I said, "Everyone is so focused on Nefertiti that they forget about Johnny. He's an innocent. He shouldn't die or be tormented because of his wife."

"Why do you think she bound herself to him?" asked Damian. "For protection. So that those as tenderhearted as you would decry her punishment."

What kind of woman would seduce and bind another to her to protect herself? She had banked on the idea that if caught, she would not be killed because her life was bound to Johnny's.

"I don't know where she is," I said. "And even if I did, I'm not sure I would tell you."

"You still look at the world through the eyes of a human. That will change over time." His gaze was thoughtful. "I underestimated you, *Liebling*," he said softly. "I shall not do so again."

Too soon dawn arrived. Tamara was sleeping, so I kissed her forehead and whispered, "Good night."

I followed Dr. Merrick to the basement, where she showed me a room with a simple cot, pillow, and blanket.

"Thanks," I said.

"You'll be safe in here," she reassured me. "Drake and Darrius are watching Tamara. She'll be okay."

We wished each other good night and she pulled the door shut behind her.

As I sat on the bed, I shuddered, just a little, at the rough feel of cotton. The pillow looked too droopy. I wished mightily for my bed, my sheets, and my pillows.

Feeling lonely, I sat down and indulged in a little moping. My body was already feeling heavy. In a few minutes, I would pass out on the cot, Egyptian cotton or not.

"*A stóirín*," said Lorcan as he sparkled into sight. He held three big pillows and the top sheet from my bed.

"Lorcan!" I was still getting used to him popping in and out of places. I got up from the bed and we replaced the bedding.

"Thank you so much."

"You are welcome. I must return to my own sleeping quarters," he said regretfully. He studied me, then asked, "You have something on your mind?"

He was astute. Or he was in my mind again. "Damian told me he wants me to find Nefertiti so he can kill her. Doesn't he care about Johnny?"

Lorcan sat on the cot and patted it. "We all

care about Johnny. As a Consortium member, he has our protection."

"Did you find him?"

"Not yet." He took my hand and wound his fingers through mine. "You must not think badly of Damian. He has good reason to punish Nefertiti."

"I know. Nefertiti captured his sister. She died at a death camp."

"She also killed his pregnant wife."

"That's horrible!" I wondered why Damian hadn't told me. Obviously, he'd erected the psychic barrier to keep me from that information.

"Maria was six months pregnant with twins. When Nefertiti and her squad raided the village, Maria fought fiercely. Nefertiti herself wielded the blade that robbed Maria of her children, then of her life."

I felt sick. "Damian told me that his species was dying out. He also said that the pure lycanthropes weren't allowed to mate with the Roma."

"Maria was a royal Roma, and Damian was a royal lycan. The marriage was one of love, but also promised a new beginning for lycans. The hope was that they would propagate both species of lycans."

"Then he issued the ban?"

"When he discovered his slain wife, he saw that his unborn children were mutated. Had they gone to term, they would not have survived the birth. So he decreed that no pureblood would mate with Roma."

"I feel scared," I admitted. "If anyone could find Nefertiti, I could. Too many people want to get their hands on her for me to feel safe."

"I will see to your and Tamara's protection." He hugged me. "No one will harm you, Eva. I swear it."

I dreamed of the tower. Like the time before, I escaped the growling dangers tracking me in the dark woods. I pressed the golden rose etched on the black stone to get inside and I followed the blue orbs to the top of the stairs.

I knew what awaited me in the four-poster. All the same, I drew back the shimmery curtains.

"Your fate is sealed," the wolf said, baring his sharp fangs. "You cannot escape me."

He leapt toward me, his maw opened toward my throat.

"Stay!" I screamed.

The wolf was flung to the bed and he cowered there, whining as though I had struck him.

"Remember this," I said. "I choose my own fate."

The wolf disappeared in a puff of black smoke. In his place was a single gold rose.

Chapter 13

When I awoke in the hospital basement, I felt bereft. That damned dream! I didn't feel like that snarling creature belonged in my tower. I was glad to vanquish him. I was still searching for the one beautiful thing that would complete me. I thought of the gold rose. The symbolism couldn't be plainer: Gold rose equaled Lorcan.

I rolled off the cot and stretched. Whew. I couldn't wait to take a shower and change clothes. But first I would visit Tamara. Then I would call Alison for my pint. Oh, wait. No cell phone. I wondered if Lorcan had found my backpack.

I took the stairs to the third floor. As I eased out of the door, I found Charlie standing in the hallway waiting for me.

"Oh, hey," I said. After our last feeding experience together, I was still feeling awkward. "How are you?"

"I wanted to apologize, Eva. I don't know what happened. I would never hurt you or . . . Please, I'm really sorry." He gaze flicked to the gold rose pinned on my shirt. "I see you have a better one." Blushing, he handed me a white rose, which I accepted. I pushed away my uneasiness and smiled at him. This was Charlie—he was as harmless as a puppy. I was hungry, he was my donor, so what was the issue? I pointed at an empty room. "Is in there okay?"

The grin split his face. He eagerly entered the room and I followed, shutting the door behind us to ensure privacy.

I felt dizzy with hunger and more than ready to sink my fangs into Charlie's artery.

He waited for me on the hospital bed nearest the window. He'd turned on the light above the raised bed, but the rest of the place remained in the dark. I also noticed he'd opened the window.

Charlie was prone to feeling claustrophobic even in a large space. I wasn't surprised he wanted to feel the slight breeze.

I sat next to him, laying the rose on the bed.

"I'm really sorry about Tamara. She's a nice kid."

"I appreciate your concern, Charlie."

He leaned over and tapped his exposed neck. "I know you're hungry," he said. "If you need to take a little more than usual, that's okay."

"Thanks." The first few moments with a donor were always awkward for me. They knew the score—they were voluntary vampire food. They received excellent compensation for being our sustenance. All the same, it wasn't a profession for everyone. At least donors had a choice about whether or not to give blood. Vampires had no choice at all—either we drank blood or we starved to death.

I was starving now, so I wasted no time, holding on to his shoulders and sinking my fangs in. I drank deeply and though I had learned when to stop, I took Charlie up on his offer to enjoy a little more. Finally, I drew away, wiping off the blood spots from his neck. Thanks to the anesthetic injected from vampire fangs and the healing properties of vampire saliva, donors rarely felt pain and nearly always healed instantly.

"Thanks, Charlie." I licked my lips as my fangs receded. "Did you try a new diet? You tasted kinda . . . tangy."

He slid off the bed, looking at the floor. "I'm sorry, Eva."

"You don't have to apologize for what you eat." I smiled. "I don't apologize for what *I* eat."

Dizziness assailed me. I rubbed my temples as the world tilted. What the heck?

"Charlie . . . what's . . . happening?"

"It's okay," he reassured me. "Because you're mine. He told me so. You'll be okay, Eva. Then we can be together."

He wasn't making sense. My vision grayed as I watched Charlie fade back into the shadows. I fell sideways onto the bed, unable to feel my arms or legs.

The last thing I remembered was two piercing red eyes staring at me from the open window.

"Eva?"

I heard the voice from very, very far away. I struggled toward the sound of my name. It felt as though metal liquid surrounded me, heavy yet buoyant. *Weird.* I wanted to swim toward the person calling me, but I couldn't lift my eyelids, much less my arms.

Aren't you tired? You deserve a rest.

I stopped struggling and listened to the new voice.

"Evangeline." Lorcan again. Soft and sweet.

I didn't know which way to turn. I couldn't reach the Irish-tinged voice that said my name so tenderly. Oh, I wanted to go to him desperately. *Lorcan.*

Tsk. Tsk. So many worries, so many cares.

Where should I go? What should I do?

You're exactly where you need to be.

"Where are you, love?" I heard Lorcan again. I could almost feel him reach me, his long, pale fingers stretching toward mine. He sounded insistent and I could feel his worry. Yet it was too difficult to think, to hold on.

Ssshh. It's okay. Just . . . let . . . go.

Comforted by the other voice, I turned away from Lorcan and let the odd ocean carry me away.

"We don't have much time."

I recognized the voice. Yes, he had told me it was okay to let go. Reassurance whispered through me. *Sweet Eva. It's okay. It's all right.*

Lord-a-mercy, I felt sleepy. I managed to open my eyes, but I couldn't quite focus on the faces hovering over mine.

"We must hurry."

"Are you sure this is the wisest course of action, *mein Freund*?"

"Don't question me, Otto."

Soft, warm flesh pressed against my lips and blood seeped into my mouth. I didn't really want to drink, but reflex kicked in and I did.

"Very good, Eva. Very good."

The blood tasted strange; I gagged.

"Ssshh. Almost done. There now."

The kind voice soothed me and when I was finished drinking, I drifted away once again.

The warrior's cry woke me.

My body flopped onto a hard, bumpy surface and rolled until I smacked something very big and scratchy.

I couldn't quite fathom where I was or what had happened to me. My eyes refused to open and my head felt as though it had been stuffed with cotton, soaked in alcohol, and set on fire.

Charlie. Whatever substance he'd put into his bloodstream was meant to sedate me. Betrayal settled like a cold, hard lump in my stomach.

Oh, Charlie! How could you? More important, why would he dope himself in order to dope me? What about that encounter with the strange men hovering over me? Had I only dreamed it?

Sounds of fighting penetrated my fogged senses: grunts and growls, metal on metal, feminine shouts. As I shook off the mental ickiness, I realized my hands were bound in front of me.

This night just kept getting better and better.

Though it just about killed me to do it, I managed to pry open my eyelids.

At first, I could see nothing but shadowy objects in the dark. But my nose was working just fine. The dank smell of earth, the crisp sting of pine needles, and the acrid odor of smoke filled my nostrils. Then, as my vamp vision cleared, I could see a glade. In the middle of it was a low-burning fire and scattered all over the place were implements used for camping.

At the far edge of the campfire, I could make out Durriken and a silver-haired man fighting two vampires I didn't recognize. Their eyes glowed red and their fangs looked sharp and scary. To the left of that melee, a dark-haired woman wielded a frying pan like it was Excalibur; she was shouting in an unknown language as she smacked a very large black wolf about the head and shoulders. *Lucky?* I couldn't be sure.

My injuries were healing even as I rolled onto my side and scrabbled to my knees, but I still felt bruised and sore from head to toe. I didn't know how I'd ended up bound and thrown on the ground, but I was semi-free now. I leaned against the tree that had arrested my fall and hoisted myself to my feet.

Regular rope bound my hands, so it took only a little pulling to break the hemp and toss it to the ground. Then I staggered toward the fighting Roma, still feeling groggy.

I arrived at the edge of the clearing in time to see the older man swing his odd weapon at the vampire's neck. The gleaming blade went through skin and bone as easily as a hot knife through a stick of butter.

Oh, yuck! My gorge rose as I watched the head bounce onto the ground and roll toward me. Its surprised expression was the last thing I saw before it—and the body—burst into ash.

After watching his companion literally bite the dust, the vampire fighting Durriken spun around and fled. The boy, looking sweaty and triumphant, turned with the older gentleman toward the woman and the wolf.

As far as I could tell, he was trying to protect himself while the woman bashed at him. He dodged and leapt, yowling pitifully. The woman reminded me of an angry bee buzzing around a limp flower. I couldn't understand her words, but I guessed their gist.

Unbelievably tired, I stumbled toward them. Durriken saw me first. He hurried to me, grabbing me around the waist just as I went down. What was wrong? I couldn't shake off whatever Charlie had slipped me in his blood.

"Tell her to stop," I whispered as I leaned heavily on the boy. "Please."

"Mama!" shouted Durriken. He added a few other words and his mother, though obviously displeased, backed away from the beast.

"Take me to him." I felt as though I was going to black out again.

The man, who I assumed was Durriken's father, put down his blade and grabbed me from the other side. They took me as far as they dared.

Lucky. He always seemed to show up when I needed him. Had he tried to save me again, only to stumble upon the Roma camp?

He looked at me and whined. Familiar, those eyes. I couldn't quite pinpoint why.

Thank you. I felt my mind gray; darkness edged my consciousness. *Lucky . . .*

He barked and edged closer.

"Don't hurt him," I begged the woman, who stared at me with dark, suspicious eyes. "Please . . ."

"I do not trust *gadjikane,*" she said sharply. "You are not Roma."

"I am a mother." I smiled weakly. "Keep him . . . safe."

"Hmph!" she said. "And where do we keep you?"

I didn't have a chance to answer the question. As darkness consumed me utterly, I saw Lucky turn away and lope into the trees.

I fell softly into the opaque chasm.

Chapter 14

"S he lives!" crowed Jessica as my eyes fluttered open. She leaned over my prone body and grinned. I couldn't stretch my lips to form an answering smile. Thirst clawed at me. My throat was so dry I could barely swallow.

As she straightened, I saw Patrick standing behind her, to the left.

"Where am I?" I asked. "What happened?"

"The short version: You were knocked out, kidnapped, rescued, and you passed out. Durriken came to the hospital and got us. We brought you here." Jessica gestured around the room. "This is one of the zillion rooms on the second floor of our house. You slept straight through the rest of the night and the day."

So it was the next evening. What had Charlie ingested that had managed to drug me so thoroughly and yet not affect him? Or *had* the drug affected him? "How's Tamara?"

"Right as rain, babe. Dr. Merrick gave her the thumbs-up and released her."

I nodded. "And Lucky? I mean, the wolf?"

Patrick and Jessica exchanged a look. "Helene—Durriken's mom—said he disappeared. She said he was the biggest wolf she'd ever seen. She didn't think he was Roma or lycanthrope."

Disappointment shot through me. I hoped he was okay. He hadn't responded to my mental telepathy. But he had responded to my emotions. And he had tried to rescue me.

"Jess, I'm really thirsty."

Once again, I found myself drinking from Jessica's wrist. When I was done, I grinned. "Champagne truffles?"

"Her favorite," said Patrick, chuckling. He stepped closer. His gaze was kind. "It appears Charlie ingested phenobarbital in large enough quantities to disable you. We think he took the pills just before he entered the hospital to feed you."

"Phenobarbital? That's a little nineteen sixties, isn't it?"

Jessica shrugged. "We found a pill bottle tossed in the bushes outside of the entrance. Stan said something about enzyme induction. Basically, the guy metabolizes chemicals really fast. We don't know why he did it and we can't ask his sorry ass because he's gone."

I nodded. Charlie had drugged me, then run away. Was he in cahoots with the Wraiths? Or had he hooked up with the rogue vamp lycans? Or was it all one group of crazy people?

"Who's manning the library?" I asked.

"Tamara is showing Ralph the ropes so he can take over your duties for a while."

"A while? As in: longer than a few hours?"

"As in: longer than a few days," said Jessica. "We have to protect you and Tamara."

"You are very valuable," added Patrick. "The mansion is nearly as secure as the compound and it is far more comfortable."

"You're saying that as a pet psychic, I'm in demand?" I tried to make it into a joke, but my voice cracked. I hadn't quite come to grips with the idea that I was in danger.

"Since only you and Koschei have the ability, then yes. You are very much in demand," said Patrick.

"You won't be safe until we find those Wraith bastards," groused Jessica. "That's why Damian and one of his teams are at the library watching Tamara. They'll escort her back to the house."

I was glad to know that Tamara was being protected, but I was still confused about why anyone would want to harm either me or Tamara. I was sure a mistake had been made. The idea of being away from the library, from my home, from the life I'd built as a human and then as a vampire disturbed me even more than being drugged and kidnapped.

"We think Ron and his idiots are skulking around town," answered Jess. "And we think he knows you can talk to the animals." She snickered as she hummed the theme song to the Rex Harrison version of *Dr. Doolittle*.

"Very funny, Jess." I rolled my eyes. "What am I supposed to do around here?"

"Housework?" suggested Jessica with a wide grin. Then she patted my hand. "Sorry, sweets. I know you'll miss your books, but Lor's taken over this wing of the house and he has more books than the library of Alexandria. In fact, I think he has books *from* the library of Alexandria. Besides, I've got a project for you."

Lor was a bigger bibliophile than I was. Although getting my hands on Lor's book collection appealed to me, I shuddered to think what kind of project Jessica had in mind. "I told you that sharp knives make me nervous. No more sword lessons."

"Can I help how slippery pure fairy gold is? I said I was sorry."

During my first and last lesson with Jessica's Ruadan swords, she had accidentally pinned me to a tree by my shoulder. Good thing vampires healed fast.

"What I have in mind doesn't involve pointy objects, okay?" Jessica grinned.

That wide smile and too innocent gaze made me really nervous.

"Quit torturing me," I said as I sat up. "What nefarious plan have you cooked up, Jess?"

Jessica's eyes sparkled with excitement. "I want you to be Broken Heart's new schoolteacher."

My mind instantly spun with the possibilities—lessons and field trips and—*wait a minute.* "I can't."

Her excitement dimmed. "Why the hell not?"

"I don't have a degree. Not even a GED. I'm not qualified."

She waved a hand dismissively. "Who gives a shit about that? You're smart, you're enthusiastic, and you're a vampire. We won't have to bring in anyone from outside or try to glamour some poor human. You already do the Shakespeare Club for the teens, and you created that story program just for Ralph's twins. Plus, you know what a freaking centurion is and you say Latin words like they're fun. Let's not forget that I caught you reading the dictionary. *Nobody* reads the dictionary."

"Lor does," interjected Patrick.

"Okay, nobody except Eva and Lor read the dictionary."

"Jessica, I'm really not qualified." I couldn't believe how badly I suddenly wanted the job. Teaching the kids of Broken Heart would be nearly as wonderful as discovering Shakespeare's lost plays. I could create different curriculums—one for high school, one for elementary, one for preschool. We could do grade ranges instead of forcing the kids into specific grades. I swallowed the sigh. I hadn't known I could want something more than what I already had. My life was full of blessings. *Still . . .*

Looking at the patchwork quilt that covered me, I shook my head.

"Aw, c'mon," said Jessica. "We need you. Hey! How about I take this up with the Consortium? I'll talk ol' Ivan into it. Would you go for it then?"

A little flame of hope flickered. "If the Consortium agrees to it, Jess, then, yeah—I'd love to do it."

"Sweet! Okay, babe, we gotta go figure out what's stinking up our house," said Jess cheerfully. "The third floor reeks like a dead guy's bad breath." She fluttered her eyelashes at Patrick. "No offense, honey."

"Hmm. I suppose a breath check is in order," he said. The look he shot her left no doubt that tongue and lips would be involved with the process. "Why don't we reconnoiter upstairs and begin the procedure?"

Grinning, Jess waved good-bye to me and left. Patrick took a seat near the bed.

"She's trying to make me feel better," I said. "But we've got problems, don't we?"

"Yes, Eva." He sighed. "Through our network of informants, we've found that the Wraiths are disbanded. No one has seen Ron in weeks."

"The hybrids didn't just show up. Someone led them here."

He nodded. "The experiments done on tainted vampires and captured lycans now are very much the same as those done during World War Two."

"You're saying it's no coincidence Nefertiti has revealed herself." Realization dawned and fear chilled me. "Her reinforcements have arrived."

"And they are quite good at avoiding detection. Other than the three lycans chasing you, one of them Faustus, there are no signs of outsiders." Patrick leaned forward and patted my hand. "If there is a war coming, you will be very much in demand."

"Just because I can talk to them and hear their thoughts doesn't mean I'll be of any use. I can't control them."

"Have you tried?"

I shook my head. I was reminded of my dream where the wolf cowered at my command. I looked at Patrick and saw the speculation in his eyes. "You think I can."

"For some reason the powers of Turn-bloods bitten by Lorcan are increasing exponentially. Jessica is quite good with her swords and with flight. She is also able, with some limitations, to appear and reappear. Usually it takes centuries to progress that far."

"I can see why I would be of interest." Damian and Johnny could use me to control Nefertiti. The Consortium could use me to hear the thoughts of the lycanthropes and Roma, maybe even to control unruly prisoners. And the bad guys could use me to control their experiments.

Nausea roiled and I pressed my hand against my stomach. Oh, God. I *was* in trouble.

"I know it's a lot to grasp," soothed Patrick. "Take a moment, if you need it. Your daughter is waiting to see you."

He rose from the chair; his smile was reassuring.

I sat up slowly and felt somewhat normal. The door popped open and there was Tamara.

"Hi, Mom!"

"Hi, honey. Your lips are doing something weird," I said. "Are you aware they're curling up at the corners?"

"Ha, ha. I can smile, y'know."

Since when? Had I worried her so much that she was trying to be nice? I preferred my darling sarcast (one who uses sarcasm) to this . . . this . . . *"Jollier."*

"Ah, better a jollier than a persifleur." She chuckled. "Nice one, Mom. Ten points for you." She sat next to me and patted my leg. "You gonna live, so to speak?"

"Yeah. How about you?"

"Think so."

A knock sounded. My daughter skittered off the bed, hurried to the door, and flung it open.

Durriken waited on the other side. He bowed to me, but his gaze never strayed from Tamara. "Hello, Miss LeRoy. Are you well?"

"Yes. Thanks."

Oh, crap. Apparently, my teenage daughter had met her hero. I felt a little deflated that her smile and emotional buoyancy weren't the result of seeing that I was okay. Tamara had never shown much interest in boys or in dating. Her sixteenth birthday was two months away. I suppose I hadn't thought much about her hanging out with people her own age, since she so rarely showed interest in doing so.

When Durriken offered his arm to her as if he were about to escort a princess to the ball, my daughter wrapped her arm around his and walked to my bedside. I tried to handle this turn of events with aplomb, but I felt kinda jealous. Even though I'd had every intention of introducing Durriken to Tamara, I hadn't thought they'd become peas in a pod.

"When did you two meet?" I asked.

"Last night," said Tamara. "He and his parents brought you to the hospital and he came to check on me."

"Wow. That's great." I tried to infuse enthusiasm in my voice, but I failed miserably. Tamara looked at me with raised brows. I didn't want to embarrass her or myself by turning into a suspicious, lecturing mother. "So, what're you doing now?"

"We're going to explore the house. This place is huge." She grinned at Durriken and he looked flummoxed. He grinned back at her. Gak! They were already in the moon-eyed stage.

"Be careful. Avoid dark, small places, and check in. Often. Don't . . . uh, do anything silly. Because I'm sure Jess has this place decked out with video cameras. Lots of them."

"Whatever you say, Mom."

Tamara and I had talked about the birds and the bees many times. Granted, my mother had done the same for me, and it hadn't stopped me from losing my virginity and getting pregnant.

However, I didn't think Tamara would run off and do anything sexual (gasp, blech, aah!) with Durriken. And his mother seemed the type to hack off genitalia if she thought 'em used inappropriately. All the same, I felt worried.

"Your daughter will be safe with me," said Durriken. "I will protect Tam."

"Yeah, Mom. Nothing bad will happen to me while I'm with Durry."

Ugh. Cute-name phase had been initiated. I knew kissing and . . . and *touching* wouldn't be far behind. Tam leaned down to buss my cheek. Oh, my God. Parental affection. Who was this girl?

I smiled bravely. "Have a good time." *But not too good of a time, gosh darn it!*

They waved good-bye, and then off they went to explore Silverstone mansion. As the door clicked shut behind them, I felt very lonely. It had always been me and Tamara. She valued her independence, but she'd never been away from me. I knew that one day she'd go off on her own, but I wasn't quite ready to let her go. I didn't want her to explore the world without me.

You never have to cut the apron strings, baby. You just make 'em as long and as strong as your child needs. Then they have something to hold on to when they fall and they can follow those strings all the way home, if need be. The hardest thing to do is not hold on to the strings, to stop yourself from yanking on 'em to save your child from bad decisions. Your job as a mother is to be there with open arms. It's up to the one you raised to decide whether or not to step into your embrace.

My mother was a wise woman. Whenever I was feeling lonely for Tamara—when she went off to school or to spend the night with a friend—my mother got out the Ben & Jerry's pints and the Apron-String Lecture. She knew a thing or three about letting go—as a mother watching her child find independence and as a human being taking the journey to the next life. God, I missed her.

But I guessed it was time to start lengthening the apron strings.

When I left the room, I wandered down the hallway. I wondered where Lorcan was and what he was doing. Then I wondered where Durriken and Tamara were . . . and hoped they weren't doing anything.

The Silverstone mansion was huge and sprawling. It was no surprise to me that Lorcan had a whole wing to himself. The library was at the end of the hallway. Double doors opened to reveal the dim and dusty confines of the original library. A second, smaller one was located downstairs. That was where Jessica showed me Lor's books as well as a cache from the Consortium's traveling library.

I paused on the threshold. Wow. Ever see that scene in Disney's *Beauty and the Beast* where the Beast shows Belle the palace library? That's the way I felt when I entered this wondrous place.

The room was large and circular. Book-filled shelves lined the walls from floor to ceiling. A walkway about fifteen feet up followed the curve of the room. In the middle of the room, the shelves curved toward a tall stained-glass window. Below it, I saw a dark alcove and the shadowy outline of the staircase that led to the second "floor" of the library.

I nearly drooled.

Four large cherrywood tables with matching chairs were scattered here and there. All the tables had open books on them—as if a hurried scholar couldn't be bothered to shelve the tomes.

Curious, I looked at the books on the table nearest to me. Nearly all of them covered various topics about ancient Egyptian culture. I peered down at the pages of the open text.

O you who take away hearts and accuse hearts, who re-create a man's heart (in respect of) what he has done, he is forgetful of himself through what you have done. Hail to you, lords of eternity, founders of everlasting!

It nearly sounded like an appeal to a vampire. I looked at the cover: *Ancient Egyptian Book of the Dead.* Ah. An appeal to ancient gods—not to the fanged ones. I returned the book to its original position. The other hardbacks on the table included subjects about Seth, the god of chaos, ancient Egyptian spells, and one about the lost world of the Sudan. The Consortium had archaeologists in the Sudan trying to dig up a temple. I knew it had something to do with the origins of the taint—and maybe even finding the cure. While the vampire disease had existed for as long as vampires had walked the earth, it had seen a resurgence in recent years, becoming almost plaguelike in its duration and intensity. The Consortium, the Wraiths, and even the Council of Ancients had been affected by the illness and all were searching for a way to stop it.

Rumor had it that the leader of the Wraiths might've unleashed the disease into parakind simply as a method of biological warfare. It seemed Ron wanted more than just to wipe out the Consortium—he wanted to wipe out the Ancients, too. But his plan must've backfired somehow. All vampires were affected by the disease, even the Wraiths.

Creeped out by the idea of such a terrible disease, I returned my attention to the library. On the left side was a huge stone fireplace. Two red velvet wingback chairs sat in front of the fireplace; each had a matching red velvet footstool. I walked to one of the chairs and ran my palm over it. Soft and worn. Probably original furniture. Each chair had an oval cherrywood side table with a tall lamp, tilted at the right angle for reading.

I couldn't resist the idea of sitting in one of these chairs and whiling away the evening reading books. What else was I supposed to do? Usually I was at the Broken Heart library, tending to all the tasks there. My daughter was exploring a big, spooky house with a potential boyfriend. My friends were checking each other's nonexistent breath. Yet I still felt guilty about curling into a comfy chair and indulging my reading obsession. I looked up, up, up at all the books. When would I ever have another opportunity to enjoy this place?

Giddy, I decided to wander along the walkway and see what treasures awaited me there. As I stepped into the darkest part of the alcove, a hand reached out and grabbed my forearm.

"Hey! What the—"

Chapter 15

"Jeez, Eva," said Ralph. "It's just me."

He pulled me close to the window. My eyesight adjusted. His hair was medium brown, cut short, his eyes were blue, and he wasn't quite as tall or buff as Lorcan. Ralph was lean and wiry. He looked like a working man, which I appreciated.

"I dropped by to see how you were doing."

"You scared me."

"I'm sorry."

An awkward silence ensued. Well, it was probably awkward for me. I wasn't sure what else to say. I found myself staring at the stained glass again. The only image taking up the entire window was one long-stemmed red rose.

"I wanted to know if—if you wanted to go see a movie." He pointed at the floor. "Downstairs. They're playing *Casablanca*. I've been told approximately forty-two times that you can't leave." He looked at me, his blue eyes sincere. "Why not?"

"I was sorta kidnapped."

"Are you okay?" He grasped my arm. "Did they hurt you?"

"No, I'm all right." I felt uncomfortable with Ralph intruding on my personal space. "Thanks for taking care of the library, Ralph. I appreciate it."

"It's no problem." He stepped closer, his eyes filled with empathy. "I'm glad you're okay, Eva." He leaned down and kissed my cheek.

"What the bloody hell is going on?"

Startled, I looked up—straight into the angry gaze of Lorcan.

"None of your concern," answered Ralph. I saw annoyance flash in his eyes.

Lorcan's jaw clenched and his hands curled into fists. Fury vibrated off him. *She's mine. Stay away from her. Damn it!*

Yikes. I could hear Lor's thoughts, but he probably didn't realize that I could hear him now. Jessica and Patrick shared each other's thoughts, but most mind-speak was reserved for emotionally attached vamps.

Ralph wrapped an arm around my shoulders. "I was asking Eva to the movies."

Obviously frustrated, Lorcan stared at me. I saw a muscle ticking in his jaw.

"I'm sorry, Ralph," I said. "I can't go with you."

He looked at me, looked at Lorcan, and then sighed. "I see."

I felt bad. Ralph was a wonderful man. Not only was he handsome and nice, but he understood the vampire lifestyle. He was a rarity. For me, though, Ralph couldn't compare to Lorcan.

"Bye, Eva." He offered Lorcan his hand. Lorcan shook it. "Lorcan."

"Ralph."

I watched Ralph leave, then turned my gaze to Lorcan. As always, he was dressed in black, but he was casual Goth tonight. He wore a black T-shirt and black jeans and black Converses. His dark hair had been pulled into a queue. Jessica called Patrick "Remington Steele" because he reminded her of Pierce Brosnan. I had to admit that the O'Halloran brothers resembled my favorite 007.

Lorcan's gaze was dark and dangerous. He stalked me until I was backed against the window. Adrenaline spiked in my stomach as he stood before me, studying me. Then he grasped my hands and brought each wrist to his lips for a soft kiss.

"You are well?" he asked softly.

"Uh-huh." I couldn't articulate more than that. He looked beautiful and angry and yummy.

Heat pooled between my thighs and desire thickened hotly through me. I wasn't sure what to do. The excitement of sexual longing hadn't happened since Michael seduced my foolish seventeen-year-old self. I'd had two lovers since then, but had derived very little pleasure from those encounters. My last boyfriend, who had to date me for nearly six months before he got into my pants, called me frigid. Not long after we broke up, my mother was diagnosed with terminal cancer. I had one relationship—brief and unremarkable—before Tamara and I moved to Broken Heart.

Lorcan inspired bone-melting lust. His tongue flickered across my pulse-deprived wrist. Tingles of longing skipped up my arm.

His gaze captured mine. "Do you want me to stop?"

No. Yes. I don't know. I shook my head.

He raised my arms and pressed them against the window. I could feel the beveled glass against the back of my hands as his palms flattened against mine. Toe-to-toe, he covered my body with his, pushing my breasts into his muscled chest. My nipples enjoyed this situation so much that they tried to drill into his skin. And he knew it, too. He closed his eyes, shuddering, and when he opened them again, I knew I was done for.

His lips descended to mine.

My body was a tinderbox and Lor was the match. We burned hot and bright, but ours wasn't a spark quickly doused. Given the opportunity, the flames would build and grow and strengthen. In that moment, I knew that I wanted Lorcan—in every way that counted.

He kissed me passionately. Desperately. I melted all over again. Would every kiss be this way between us? He dropped my arms and gathered me into his embrace, holding me against him as his tongue warred with mine. I reveled in his loss of control.

Heat and light filled me. I wiggled closer,

moaning as he attacked my mouth with renewed fervor. I pulled him closer still.

God, he was beautiful.

I never felt so . . . so wonderful. I felt as though I had come home. I was in the arms I had always longed for, with the man I had always wanted.

"I promised to protect you," he said sorrowfully. "And I failed."

"No," I said. "Never."

"I have cared for no one as I care for you. I do not have the words to describe how you make me feel. I never want to lose you, Eva."

"You won't," I said. Desire raged through me. I lifted his shirt and stroked his stomach.

"I would bind with you," he murmured against my lips. "For us, a hundred years would pass as if it had been a day."

"You're crazy," I said, but my heart jolted. Was Lor saying he'd marry me? He was such a poet. Such a lovely, sweet poet. "Shouldn't we date first?"

"Anything you wish," he murmured.

He was kissing me dizzy. Really dizzy. I felt faint. Reluctantly, I pulled back. "Lor, I feel strange."

"Me, too. You drive me mad."

"Ditto. But this is something different." My whole body went cold, then hot. My stomach clenched and my head squeezed. Darkness roared at me. I saw Lor's shocked expression right before I passed out.

When I opened my eyes, I saw Jessica. Sheesh. This was really getting to be a pattern.

"I'm sorry, Eva. I'm so fucking sorry."

"What are you talking about? What's happened now?"

I saw Patrick next to Jessica, his gaze filled with sorrow.

"Oh, my God. Tamara."

"She's fine," reassured Jess. "She's in the kitchen with Durriken and Helene's sitting between them."

If my daughter was okay, then what was the issue? "Did the library burn down?"

"No. Ralph has that handled."

Well, then, if Tamara was safe and my home was safe, that meant *I* must be the cause of my friends' concern.

My heart squeezed. Had Charlie given me something that was worse than drugged blood? He was a human. I was a vampire. Supposedly, as one of the undead, I had a godlike immune system.

"I fainted," I said. "Isn't that an odd thing for a vampire to do?"

"Well, yeah. Sorta." Jessica looked uncomfortable and twitchy. Patrick put his arm around her and drew her close.

I was torn between demanding the truth and delaying hearing the bad news. My stomach felt lined in lead. Whatever they had to tell me, I was sure it didn't involve winning the lottery or discovering a lost Shakespeare play.

My gaze swept the space. This wasn't the same room I'd had before. I couldn't pinpoint why the decor, or rather the lack of it, bothered me.

The door clicked open, stalling the bad news. Lorcan slipped inside.

Lorcan's gaze captured mine. His eyes reminded me of storm clouds, especially with those raven eyebrows always dipped into twin frowns.

"Evangeline."

He adorned my name with such tenderness that I felt an unaccountable need to weep. I couldn't explain the feelings that overtook me. I was just so glad to see him, to know that he was near. He coasted to the other side of the bed, picked up my hand and kissed my knuckles. My skin trembled under the softness of his lips.

"*A stóirín,*" he murmured. He glanced at Jessica and Patrick. "I will tell her."

Jess and Patrick nodded, their gazes filled with concern and, if I was any judge, fear. I watched them leave. As the door shut with a metallic thud, I suddenly realized why I had been bothered by the room's setup.

It reminded me more of Faustus's cell than of hospitable accommodations. I had no doubt it was locked from the outside. Were they protecting me from another kidnapping attempt? Or were they protecting others from me?

I didn't think I'd like the answer.

"I'm thirsty." I licked my lips. "Jess fed me, too."

"That was yesterday evening," he said. "You've slept through again, Eva."

"I seem to be doing that a lot lately." I sighed. "It wasn't the drugs that did me in this time."

"No. We took you to Stan and kept you unconscious to run tests."

Had it been capable, my heart would've leapt out of my chest. My mother, tired and pale for weeks, passed out at work. I took her to the hospital emergency room. The doctor was friendly but patronizing, too. *We'll keep her overnight, run some tests. Probably just stress and exhaustion. Don't worry, Miss LeRoy.*

When I returned the next morning, my mother told me the truth. Terminal cancer. No surgery, no radiation, no drugs could arrest the disease. Two months later, she was gone.

My eyes ached with the need for tears. Had someone taken a torch to my throat? It felt dry and crispy. I wanted liquid. I wanted blood. "Is there a donor available?"

"We cannot give you a donor." He cupped my hand in both of his. "But we are looking into an alternative food source for you."

My stomach did a slow dive to my toes. "Oh, God. Lor, what did Charlie do to me?"

"When you were taken from the hospital, do you remember anything prior to stumbling into the Roma camp?"

I nodded. "I had an odd dream that someone opened his wrist and made me drink his blood. It didn't taste right."

"*Damnú air.*" His grip tightened. "My darling Evangeline." He pressed his cheek against my hand. He looked at me, sorrow filling his gaze. "You have the taint."

Chapter 16

*T*he prince walked west. In every village along the road, he asked about the beautiful maiden, but none had seen a woman such as he described. Weeks passed and still the prince did not find either his soul mate or the help promised by the fortune-teller.

Finally the prince reached the edge of the continent. He could go west no longer—not unless he chartered a ship. That evening, he lodged at an inn built into a seaside cliff overlooking the gray ocean. From his balcony, the prince watched lightning dance among dark clouds. He knew the brewing storm would be a nasty one and he decided to sup early so that he could return to the safety of his room before the weather turned foul.

Then he heard the dulcet tones of a woman singing. Entranced by the lovely voice, he flew from the inn to the beach below. There he found a young lady sitting on a rock, staring into the sea. Her dress was black and her blond hair covered by black lace. Her song was very sad and her tears fell like tiny diamonds onto the sand.

"Why are you weeping?" he asked.

"Our family has suffered greatly from the plague," she said. "My father and my two youngest sisters died this very week. I've been spared only because I've been away at school. My elder sister took care of everyone, though she is very ill herself. Now she lies alone in our cottage, suffering greatly.

"A neighbor sent word about my family's deaths and my sister's terrible illness. I've been traveling ever since, hoping to reach home so that I may be with my sister. She is such a good soul, so beautiful and kind."

The prince took pity on the young woman. "I will take you to her. How far away is your home?"

"Two days' walk from the inn. I would go onward except that bandits and evil spirits roam the woods at night."

"Do not worry, pretty one. I will help you." The

prince used his glamour to hypnotize the girl. He took from her neck only what he needed, then gathered her into his arms and rose into the air.

Thunder boomed as the storm drew closer, but the prince flew through the night, reaching the little farm just before dawn. He took the sleeping girl into the barn and settled her into a pile of warm, soft hay. She dared not enter the house yet, not until measures were taken to rid the cottage of the plague.

With only minutes until dawn, the prince entered the cottage and sought the bedroom of the dying sister. When he opened the door, he saw a woman asleep on her pallet, her skin pallid and her breathing erratic. She had hair the color of a raven's wings and lips as red as the rose. But it was not her ravaged beauty that called to him. It was the instant connection of his soul to hers. She was the one he had waited for—she was his other half, his truest love.

The prince dropped to his knees and wept.

He had found his maiden.

And she was not long for this world.

—From *The Prince and the Maiden*,
an unpublished work by
Lorcan O'Halloran

Chapter 17

When my mother was dying from cancer, I read everything about disease and medicine and psychology that I could get my hands on. I think, in some corner of my mind, I was hoping to find a way to save her.

On one of my many trips to the library, I picked up *On Death and Dying* by Elisabeth Kübler-Ross. In the book, the author described the five stages of grief. I read it hoping to prepare myself for losing my mother.

What I didn't know, or maybe what I didn't accept, was that nothing could prepare me for

Mom's death. I had always turned to books, to knowledge, to help me get through everything in my life—and, sometimes, to escape it. But grief was a journey through a forest of razor blades. I walked through every painful inch of it—no shortcuts and no anesthesia.

My mother had taught me that life is about choices. Sometimes things go your way, and sometimes they don't. But you always have a choice about how to act and how to feel.

"Eva?"

I blinked. I had mentally wandered away from Lor the minute he pronounced my death sentence. How would I tell Tamara? Who would care for her if I . . . ? I couldn't wrap my brain around the idea of my own death. It was one thing to have the Grim Reaper sneak up on you and another thing entirely to get his engraved invitation.

Even as questions and worries battered at my mind, I thought about *On Death and Dying*. The first stage of grief was denial. I didn't have to argue with Lor or Stan or the science. I had the taint. Okay, then, I'd just skip denial and go right on to being gloriously pissed off.

"Did Charlie give me the taint? Is that why I can't have a donor?" Anger made me feel stronger. I sat up in the bed. Then I realized I was wearing a hospital gown and nothing else. Zarking fardwarks! Just who had stripped off my clothes before allowing the scientist to poke and prod me?

"No human has ever been a carrier for the taint, but we aren't taking any chances. We don't know who kidnapped you and we don't know why he—or she—poisoned you."

"But whoever it is knows that I can communicate with lycans."

"Yes, that's very likely. But why would he give you the taint?"

"He wants to destroy the one person who could stop his evil plans involving vamp lycans." The mystery bad guy was also cruel. Why give me a debilitating disease that would kill me slowly when removing my head would accomplish the same end?

"Lor, I drank from Jess yesterday. Is she . . . you know . . . okay?"

"She doesn't have the taint."

Thank God. I inhaled through my nose and out through my mouth. When I was human, deep breathing often helped me to de-stress and clear my mind. It didn't help this time. Breathing, deeply or otherwise, just felt weird.

"God! Why me? Why?"

Lor seemed to understand that I didn't need him to respond. I ranted and raved for a few minutes more, not even able to make sense of my own words. But my emotions I understood.

I didn't want to die. Not again.

"I was looking forward to immortality," I said, pressing my palms against my aching eyes. "I was finally getting used to a nighttime schedule, too."

"Eva, don't."

I heard the quake in his voice and my hands dropped heavily to the bed. I looked at him. "Don't what?"

"Don't be brave. Don't be funny. Or understanding. Or kind."

His silver eyes gleamed with emotions I couldn't define. His jaw clenched and his lips pressed together. Oh. I got it then. He wanted me to be furious. He wanted me to punish him with my rage. His guilt demanded it. I thought of him like a moth—attracted to the light, only to be harmed by its beauty, its heat. Did he want to be around me, only to be so eaten up by remorse and sorrow that he couldn't stand to be near me?

So what it boiled down to was that Lor felt responsible. If he hadn't drained me and left me to die, then I wouldn't have the taint. I would be alive. I would be human. I was sure he had similar thoughts about all the Turn-bloods. Maybe their lives would be different, would be better, if not for him. As long as he held that belief about himself and others, there would never be any healing—not for Lor, and not for the rest of us.

"How long are you going to flay yourself for acts over which you had no control?"

His mouth dropped open. "What?"

"You were turned into a mindless, starved beast. You did what most mindless, starved beasts do—you tracked down food and you noshed. If you'd been in your right mind, you wouldn't have done it."

"It's not that simple."

"Yes, it is." I grabbed his T-shirt and pulled him close. "Forgive yourself."

"Eva, I can't just—"

I yanked him closer and he let me do it.

"Have you tried?" I asked.

He shook his head, looking bemused. I knew he was stronger and faster, but I didn't care. My immortal life was going to end. There was no more time for planning or worrying or contemplating. Before I passed on, I would help Lor through his razor-blade forest—whether he wanted me to or not.

He looked at me uncertainly, his lips twitching. Amusement flashed in his eyes, but was soon lost in the serious monk's expression he'd probably spent centuries perfecting.

"You're stubborn," I pronounced. Then I mashed my lips to his.

I kissed him desperately until I realized I probably shouldn't be kissing anyone. I let go. "The taint—I'm sorry."

"I can't get it again. My DNA was essentially changed by the radical cure. If the taint, in any form, gets into my bloodstream, my mutated antibodies will kill it."

"Okay then." I threw my arms around his neck and dipped my tongue inside his mouth. His arms went around me and he drew me from the bed, holding me against him as his tongue danced with mine. *I would bind with you, Lor. I really would.*

"Eva," he murmured. "My darling Eva. Our binding would be lovely."

I realized he had responded to my thoughts. I pulled away, just a little, and asked, "Why can you hear what I'm thinking?"

I wished immediately that I hadn't asked. He gently put me on the bed and tucked me back under the sheet. He straightened his clothes, but he couldn't fix the tousled look of his hair or hide his swollen lips. When he stepped away from the bed, away from *me*, I felt the loss keenly. Obviously, I had shaken him . . . but he had shaken me, too. To the core. I still felt internal earthquakes.

"I will not let you die," he said. "I owe you that much." I heard the grief and recrimination in his words. I wanted to hug him *and* punch him.

"I'm not a debt," I said, sighing. My hunger reasserted itself and I rubbed my tummy. The only thing I wanted more than food was . . . Lorcan.

"I will bring you sustenance."

Apparently only one of my hungers would be assuaged. I plucked at the thin sheet covering my body and wished mightily that I had the gumption to jump Lor's bones. Although I would never bind to him now, I would miss the opportunity to try a *little* hanky-panky.

A hungry vampire knows no shame. When Lor brought me the Great Dane, I managed only a token protest. The dog leapt onto my bed and lay down next to me. His fur was dark brown with splotches of black. Lor had shaved a spot on the dog's neck, which made it easier to sink my fangs into his skin.

I didn't poke at his mind until I had finished drinking. He seemed content to be a vampire snack. Like those of most dogs, his thoughts and feelings were simple. He liked how I smelled and he wanted a nap. And he really wanted a ham bone.

"His blood tastes different." I didn't want to say "awful," because doing so would not only dishonor Lor's attempts to help me but would also insult the dog.

"It's not ideal," said Lor. "Animal blood will not sustain you indefinitely. You need circulating human blood to maintain your health."

"And how am I supposed to get that?"

"We're testing donors. It is possible, though very unlikely, that a new strain of the taint can be carried by humans and we don't want you to infect innocents. If that turns out to be the case, we will have to rethink our food supply. Stan's been working on a way to create synthetic blood, but truthfully, he hasn't come up with a version that's been a long-term successful substitute."

"You're full of good news," I said. "And is this dog kept for feeding purposes? Or experimentation?"

"No. He's a stray. Don't tell Jessica, but I give him scraps. Sometimes he goes on walks with me."

The idea that he'd found a pet was endearing to me. I hadn't imagined Lor hanging out with a big ol' dog. "What's his name?"

"I call him Bert."

It was such an un-dog-like name that I smiled. Lor smiled back. "I meant to ask if anyone was feeding the animals while I'm gone."

"They don't come when you're not there," replied Lorcan. "I'll bring you some books from the library, okay?"

"Why can't I go with you? That way I can choose what I like."

With Lor's encouragement, the dog leapt off my bed and padded to the door. "I'm sorry, Eva. You cannot leave this room. We can't risk it. You could infect other vampires."

"But not dogs?"

"Very unlikely."

"You don't know when I'll go loopy, do you?"

"No. The taint affects each vampire differently, but being a young Turn-blood . . . It may work faster on you than on a vampire centuries older."

"Then I definitely don't want Tamara in here."

"You're incapable of harming those you love. Haven't you claimed her? Put her under your protection?"

"Of course." I shook my head. "I can't risk it, Lor. Not even for a second would I put that child in jeopardy."

"If that is your wish."

Oh, he had no idea what kind of wishes I had. Contemplating the end of your existence made you long for every book you hadn't read, every boy you hadn't kissed, every person you hadn't apologized to, and every trip you hadn't taken.

He opened the door and Bert sauntered through it first. Lor gave me one last smile and then the heavy metal clanked shut behind him.

I was left in my prison with only my thoughts . . . and my fears.

Chapter 18

As the days passed, I felt more and more lethargic. Despite Stan's best efforts, he was unable to create a suitable synthetic blood or to discount donors as possible taint carriers. As much as I adored Bert, his blood was not nourishing. I felt as though I was a puzzle with a piece or two taken out of the whole every day. Soon there would be no pieces left.

Lor brought me books. When I grew too tired to read, he read stories to me. His voice was beautiful and he really brought on the Irish to entertain me. He would've made a fine actor, but I knew his performances were for an audience of only one—for *me.* He never missed a visit and he stayed for hours, amusing me with anecdotes or showing me bits of his writing to ask my opinion. Sometimes he just held my hand as I drifted in and out of consciousness.

We didn't soul-kiss or speak about binding. As much as I would've loved to play smoochy-face with Lor, it wasn't fair to act on our feelings.

I missed Tamara dreadfully, though she sent notes and bad jokes and funny drawings to me several times a day. Then Lor brought me a video-camera phone so I could see her face as I talked to her using the speaker function. Though I could tell she was worried about me, she still had that spark in her eye—and I attributed it to the flush of first love. Oh, I wanted the world for my baby. I hoped that for however long they had together, Durriken and Tamara would be happy. Well, that's how I wanted to feel. Mostly, I worried about my teenage daughter being so near a teenage boy. My only comfort was that Helene had become a vigilant chaperone, much to the kids' chagrin.

I tried to be brave and to emulate my mother, who carried the burden of her illness fully. She didn't want us to be weighed down with her pain or her worries. Only now did I comprehend how much suffering and how much fear she had kept from us. Or maybe Mom hadn't been afraid of her illness or of dying.

But I was.

One evening, after Bert had fulfilled his meal-ticket duty and lay contentedly next to me, Lor revealed a spectacular surprise: a thick leather-bound volume. When he opened it, I nearly went into bibliophile orgasm. The pages were like those of medieval manuscripts—handwritten meticulously in a beautiful script. Each gilded page was painted with gorgeous flowers, mythical creatures, and other fantastic images.

"Some of my original works, before computers," said Lorcan.

"Better than Microsoft Word," I murmured as I drew my finger along the thick parchment. "What language is it?"

"Magic," he said. He whispered in Gaelic. Then handwriting glimmered gold and suddenly I could read the pages.

"That is the coolest!" I read the title at the top of the page: " 'Legends of the Ancients, Ruadan the First.' "

"All the stories of the six vampires are in here," he said.

"I thought there were seven Ancients."

"There are. When the first council convened more than four thousand years ago, my father and the six vampires he made created the rules and the binding magic to keep their children, born and made, in line. Every hundred years, the council meets to revise the policies and procedures, hear grievances, render judgments, issue edicts, and so forth."

"What do vampires with grievances do between council meetings? A hundred years is a long time to hold a grudge, even for a vampire."

Lorcan chuckled. "Each Ancient handles a certain section of the world. Vampires must go to their Family headquarters with their problems. If a problem makes it all the way to the hundred-year meeting, it's like a case going before the Supreme Court."

"That makes sense." Even though I knew it wasn't close to sunrise, I still felt really tired. Bert whined, lifted his head, and licked my hand. I petted him and he snuffled, then returned to his nap. "But what happened to the seventh Ancient?"

"Three thousand years ago, he went to ground. The Ancients issued what amounted to a memo saying that Amahté had chosen to rest and when the time was right, he would return to the world. In his place stepped his blood-son, Khenti, who was turned vampire like me and Padraig."

"Didn't your dad tell you why Amahté really went to ground? Or maybe he's dead."

"We know that he's not. We have no idea what would happen if an Ancient was killed, Eva. Each Family is interconnected with their abilities and their magic. If the originator passed from this realm, it might be the end of the entire Family."

"Not good," I said. My thoughts drifted like the gel bubbles in a lava lamp: slow and wobbly, bumping into each other and getting stuck. "Amahté is in the Sudan. That's the hubbub there, right?"

"We're trying to find his temple," admitted Lorcan. "Though we seemed to have stumbled on a site dedicated to Seth—the Egyptian god of chaos. We believe Amahté might've been the first to get the taint and may have created the cure. But our efforts are slow going. The dig has suffered continual setbacks, not the least of which are sabotage and murder."

"The Ancients probably don't like the idea that you're poking around."

"We have Khenti's permission, so there's not much the council can do." He sounded so defiant, I smiled.

"So, you got the stories of six of the first vampires. That must've been interesting research."

"I interviewed them all and bugged them incessantly until I was sure I got everything right. Still, I wonder if choosing a fairy-tale format was the way to tell the stories."

Lorcan suffering from a writer's insecurities struck me as silly. Here was a man whose career spanned four millennia. I'm sure he'd had all the time he needed to perfect his craft.

"Read it to me," I asked.

He sat in the wingback, put the tome on his lap, and said, " 'Once there was a great warrior-magician whose name was Ruadan. To know a man, you must know his story, and all the stories of men begin with their mothers. . . .' "

On the story went: Bres, an immortal king who wanted to win back Eire—even to the detriment of his sons. His wife, Brigid, an immortal queen who wanted nothing more than peace for her people and for her family to be safe. But Bres lost the war and Brigid lost her sons. All but one . . .

" 'Morrigu heard the keening of her daughter,

so she turned into a crow and flew to the land of the Fomhoire. Though the dark queen craved chaos over tranquillity and war over peace, she felt pity for her daughter and offered one chance for Brigid to regain her son.

" 'Give Ruadan a cup of my blood, but be warned! When he awakes, he will not live as a man, but as a *deamhan fola.* He will never again walk in the light. He will not consume food or drink, but shall siphon the blood of the living. Neither will he have breath nor beat of heart. Never will he sire another child by his own seed.' "

In desperation, Brigid agreed to the terms of the spell—or curse, depending on your point of view. That night Morrigu turned her grandson into the first vampire. Ruadan awoke and returned to his family, but his wife went mad. Rather than be married to a monster and allow her sons to be raised by him, she planned to kill herself and their twin sons, Patrick and Lorcan.

Ruadan stopped her and convinced her to go to Eire with Brigid. For twenty-five years, he wandered the earth, making six more master vampires, before the need to see his sons overcame him. Unfortunately, his arrival in the small seaside village brought terrible consequences.

His wife killed herself and the villagers killed Patrick.

"'As his son passed from the mortal realm, Ruadan drained him and, tearing open the vein in his own neck, forced his son to drink his tainted blood. And so Padraig was Turned,'" read Lorcan in his rich voice. His brogue was deep and lyrical. "'Ruadan took Padraig to the cave where Lorcan lived and bid him to care for his brother. He instructed Lorcan on the ways of the *deamhan fola*, and warned him that his brother was no longer a man but a creature destined to walk only in the night.

"'But Lorcan did not heed his father's warnings. When Padraig awoke, he was mad with grief and hunger. He tore open his brother's neck and drained him to the point of death. When he realized what he'd done, Padraig saved Lorcan in the same manner Ruadan had saved him.

"'Now both of Ruadan's sons were *deamhan fola*.'"

When he was finished, I clapped. "Bravo! Bravo!" I pressed my hands against my heart. "You did a great job, Lor."

He smiled shyly, as though he wasn't sure how to respond to praise. "There are days that it's still strange to know that my family started the vampire race. My great-grandmother Morrigu is very powerful and truthfully, she scares the bloody hell out of nearly everyone."

"I hope never to meet her," I said, yawning. "No offense."

"None taken, especially since I feel the same way."

"How long did it take you to forgive Patrick?"

Lorcan blinked. "For what?"

"For murdering you and making you into a vampire."

Shock etched his features. "There was nothing to forgive. He was starved and didn't understand his new nature. He wasn't in his right mind."

"Sounds familiar."

"Eva . . . it's not the same as what I did. I've lived for four thousand years—that's more life than most get. It was selfish of me to try anything, to *do* anything in order to keep it."

"It's not wrong to want to live," I said quietly. "Whether you're forty or four thousand."

"Eva." He leaned forward and squeezed my arm. "You will not die. I won't let that happen. But as for me . . . If I had simply accepted my

fate, I would've saved the lives of eleven innocents."

"And Marybeth?" The only daughter of
Linda, Stan's not-girlfriend, she had been killed
by another lycan hybrid. Lorcan had saved her
life by Turning her.

He snapped the book shut. "Do not do an im-
moral thing for moral reasons!"

"Thomas Hardy," I said. "No evil can happen
to a good man, either in life or after death."

"Plato. But . . . the yoke a man creates for himself by wrong-doing will breed hate in the kind-
liest nature."

"George Eliot." I pursed my lips, thinking.
Then I grinned. "When choosing between two
evils, I always like to try the one I've never tried
before."

"What?"

"Mae West." I looked at Lorcan, wishing I
could hold him in my arms and show him he
was worthy of forgiveness and of love. "Here's
a little armchair psychology. It's easier to mentally flail yourself and stay away from those you
hurt. If you never forgive yourself, you don't
have to risk that those you killed *won't* forgive
you."

"You're saying that I'm afraid to face what I did and make peace with it."

I nodded.

"I will consider your words," he said.

I could tell by his expression that he meant what he said. I had given him something to chew on, and I was glad. Maybe, just maybe, he could build a real life in a community that would, I was certain, welcome him.

Lorcan leaned forward and tapped Bert's hip. "C'mon, boy. We need to let Eva sleep."

"I'm not tired," I whined. "I want to hear another story. What about Koschei? I'd be interested to know more about my Family."

Bert stood on all fours, shook himself so hard that drool flew everywhere, and jumped off the bed. I wiped off my slimed cheek and laughed. The Great Dane looked at me, pushed the image of a ham bone into my mind, and barked. "He wants a—"

"Ham bone," said Lor. "He has a one-track mind. He'll get one, along with the ham."

"What about the story?" I asked. I didn't want him to go. Being left alone drove me batty. I had everything in the way of entertainment, from the flat-screen TV to PlayStation 3, but I rarely used either. I hadn't thought I'd ever tire of books, but I felt restless and bored every time I picked one up. My skin itched and I felt like a thousand ants marched up and down my body. I tried not to react to the sensations.

"*Solas*," whispered Lorcan.

Pink, gold, and red orbs glittered into the room. They floated like chubby fairies above me, twinkling and swirling. Delighted, I watched them dance and play. Suddenly I felt better.

"The book will read to you," said Lor. "Close your eyes and listen. And try to rest."

"Okay." I agreed reluctantly, not energetic enough to ask questions about a book that could talk. More *sidhe* magic from Lor, no doubt.

I yawned again and lay flat, tucking myself more comfortably under the thick quilt. I watched him place the open book on his chair. He pressed his palms to it and muttered. The book glowed.

Leaning down, Lorcan kissed my forehead. I caught his face and put my mouth to his. Warmth and need flooded me instantly, but Lor's kiss was too gentle, too brief. He brought the quilt to my chin and then he turned away. He flicked off the lights, whispered good night, and he and Bert left. I sighed as the door banged shut.

I hate to be alone. Why do they leave me alone?

Clenching my teeth, I shuddered violently. If only I could breathe . . . if only I could breathe . . . *oh, you don't need to breathe, remember?* Slowly, I got hold of myself. *Everything's okay, Eva. Just chill out.*

My gaze was drawn to the glowing book. As the fairy lights engaged in a whimsical ballet in the soft darkness, Lorcan's brogue filled the room. . . .

I closed my eyes and listened.

Chapter 19

Legends of the Seven Ancients
Koschei the Second

As written by Lorcan, Filí don Tuatha de Danann
It was said that Koschei the Deathless kidnapped
women from their beds and killed men with only his
stare. Others told of a skeletal man with black hair
and wild eyes that stole brides from their husbands on
the wedding night. Some said that his soul was hid-
den inside an egg stored in a chest without a key. And

there were those who said that Koschei was merely a ghost, a harbinger of bad luck.

But Koschei was not a ghost, a kidnapper, or a soulless creature.

He was deamhan fola.

After Ruadan the First was banished by his wife, he traveled by boat to a cold and barren place far from the land of Eire. As his nature dictated, he drank the blood of mortal beings. Doing so was arduous because no victim was willing. Though Ruadan was clever and brave, he was unable to convince mortals that he was not a monster. In every village, he had to lie in wait for the unwary and take his sustenance by force. Soon Ruadan gained a reputation as a strigoi mort—*a vampire.*

Word about the strigoi mort *spread quickly. Villagers and farmers begged their gods, their wise men, and their healers for protection, but though they laid herbs on their doorsills and curses around their houses, Ruadan was not affected. Superstition was not magic; he knew the power, beauty, and truth of real magic.*

One night, Ruadan attacked a farmer, who fought so fiercely that Ruadan let him go. Though the vampire fled, the farmer and other terrified villagers chased him relentlessly. Forced to travel deeper and deeper into the craggy, snow-filled mountains,

Ruadan subsisted on animal blood and slept in caves.

Three days passed. On the fourth evening, he discovered a small village tucked into the mountainside. Cold and hungry, he managed to subdue a young woman long enough to drink what he needed. But she was the favorite wife of a powerful wizard named Koschei. Vowing revenge, Koschei used his magic to track Ruadan down.

Koschei had a more fearsome reputation than even a strigoi mort. He was bone thin and wore only black robes. His hair was long and dark, his eyes hard and green as jade. Through his magic and his psychic abilities, he coaxed food, entertainment, and companionship from other villages. Many people in the region feared Koschei and sent gifts to the dark wizard so that he would not leave his mountain home. And so Koschei had all that he needed to live a comfortable life, including many wives, concubines, and children.

Ruadan was surprised to find himself at the mercy of a mere mortal. Koschei's most powerful gift was the ability to glamour. Within moments, Koschei compelled Ruadan to tell all his secrets.

After hearing his enemy's stories, Koschei revealed his own secret: He was dying. He told Ruadan that he feared that his village and his family were in jeopardy, that if he died, rival peoples would attack.

"They will not fear me as a ghost," he said. "I will make a pact with you, demon. Give me immortal life and I will teach you my magic. I will show you how to draw a human to you, to drink, and to make him forget."

Ruadan agreed, though he warned Koschei that becoming a deamhan fola was a terrible risk. "I've never made another," he said, "and this may end your life that much sooner."

But Koschei was determined to become immortal. They agreed that he would teach Ruadan the magic first, in case the transformation failed.

The bargain struck, Koschei spent every evening with Ruadan showing him the ways of the mind. He showed Ruadan how to alter his voice and how to create illusions. "People believe so easily," he said. "Show them what they expect and they will not question you."

After thirty days had passed, Ruadan had learned all that he could from the wizard. On the thirty-first day, Koschei said, "It is time for you to keep your promise."

Ruadan drained his new friend of all his blood. When Koschei breathed his last, Ruadan tore open his own wrist and pressed the bleeding wound against the man's pale lips. His magicked blood flowed into the body of Koschei and soon the wizard awoke—as deamhan fola.

Koschei easily learned all the ways of the deamhan fola. Ruadan was pleased by the kindness of his friend and knew that Koschei would continue to bless those under his care.

Yet Ruadan was a restless soul and he wished to resume his travels. The night before Ruadan's parting, a great celebration was held. Dancing, drinking, and feasting went on through the night.

In the wee hours, as everyone fell into drunken sleep, the village was savagely attacked.

Though Ruadan and Koschei combined their powers to fight the unknown invaders, nearly all of the villagers were slain and the buildings burned. Koschei tried to Turn his sons, his daughters, his favorite wives, but it seemed none could survive the change.

"Help me," begged Koschei. "Save my children. Save my beloved wives."

But even Ruadan's attempts at Turning them failed. All of Koschei's wives died. One son and two daughters barely lived; Ruadan and Koschei escaped with them deep into the mountains. Koschei led them to a cave where he often stayed when hunting and they made the mortal survivors comfortable.

Koschei's son had seen only ten winters. His daughter Ina was barely seventeen. Tritsu was nearly twenty, already married with daughters of her own.

All but these five souls perished that terrible night.

Koschei's grief could not be contained. He begged Ruadan to turn his children into deamhan fola.

"Would you curse your son? He is but a boy. If you Turn him now, he will grow into manhood only in mind," said Ruadan.

Tritsu pleaded to die. She couldn't bear the thought of living without her children and her husband. Koschei held her hand and wept. "You will join your loved ones. This I promise, my daughter."

As Koschei held death vigils over his son and his elder daughter, Ruadan tended the pretty Ina. As the dawn crept over the mountains, two mortals passed into the next realm and three survivors sought rest in the dank darkness of the cave.

The next evening, Koschei continued his vigil over the ailing Ina while Ruadan returned to the village. He buried the dead and burned everything else to the ground. He bespelled the area so that neither human nor beast would enter what had once been a happy place.

After the work was done and the spells cast, Ruadan returned to the cave.

Koschei was readying to leave. He knew of a pow-

erful healer in another village. "I will take Ina to her and pray that my daughter lives."

That evening, Ruadan and Koschei parted ways.

Another deamhan fola *walked the earth.*

Koschei the Second.

Koschei the Deathless.

Chapter 20

Iawoke outside the mansion. I was dressed in pajamas and bunny slippers, shuffling along the driveway like a zombie.

It was pitch-black. Storm clouds scudded across the moon, blanking out even the stars. The night was eerily quiet. I thought of that scene from Dean Koontz's *Watchers* when a man alone in the woods is attacked by a vicious, unknown animal. It felt like that kind of hush, right before the creature emerged, menacing and snarling.

I turned toward the house. I had no idea how I'd gotten out. Or what I was doing trying to escape. I just wanted to get inside. If I could get inside, I would be safe.

I heard the soft growls and the patter of feet behind me. Within seconds, my arms were imprisoned by large, furry hands.

"Let me go!"

The vamp/lycans snarled and whirled around, dragging me down the driveway.

Stop! Now!

They stopped.

Fear knotted my throat and my stomach churned. Was Patrick right? Were my powers stronger than I had believed?

Let me go.

They dropped me. I landed on hands and knees. Shaking badly, I scrambled to my feet and turned to look at them. They returned my stare, but didn't move toward me.

Who are you?

We are no one.

"Eva!" Jessica, Patrick, Damian, and several others ran down the drive. Jessica held her swords at the ready. My world was spinning. I tried to stay upright, but I fell to my knees.

What do you want?

We want nothing.

Even though I felt like retching, I pushed into

their minds and found them . . . empty. Someone had scooped out their memories, their thoughts, and their wills. And whoever had done that had also implanted these answers.

Where is your master?

We have no master.

Patrick and Jessica kneeled beside me and helped me to stand. "They're just . . . shells."

Damian and his security team surrounded the creatures, pointing guns and swords at them. They growled louder, their feet scraping impatiently at the concrete. I heard their thoughts: *Kill anyone who gets in your way.*

Simultaneously, they whirled, arms extended and claws slashing.

"Stop!" I yelled and thunder reverberated in my voice. The lycans ceased their attack. I felt every pair of eyes on me.

"Eva?" Damian's voice was low, questioning.

I wanted to weep. "Their minds are gone. You must do—" I felt my throat close and I cleared it roughly. "You must do the kindest thing."

He nodded. The guns rattled efficiently and the vamp/lycans fell to the driveway, blood trickling from their wounds to stain the concrete.

"Where's Lorcan?" I asked, my voice raw.

"I am here," he whispered. He appeared behind me and swept me into his arms. I felt a tingling, then *POP!* we were in my bedroom. He tucked me under the covers, then sat next to me, brushing my hair with his long fingers.

"What did they want with me?"

Lorcan shook his head. "I do not know." His gaze blazed with fury. "But I will find out."

A few days passed and I heard nothing more. Either no one knew why I had been kidnapped a second time or they were all trying to protect me.

I'm not sure when I realized that I was dying. Maybe no one wanted to admit it. Everyone had hope. I knew from the number of visitations and the number of blood vials Stan syringed that he was working nonstop on a cure. Jessica and Patrick came every day and talked to me like I would return to my library and to my life with Tamara. I pretended that I believed everything would be all right, but after two weeks my body was so achy, so weary, and my mind so filled with fluttering, gray thoughts, I couldn't believe that I would survive.

I supposed that I had gone through all five stages of grief, but honestly, I hadn't paid attention. Did exhaustion in mind, body, and soul equal acceptance of death? I didn't know. I was scared. In those few hours that I spent alone with no one to talk to and nothing to occupy me, terror filled me until I almost choked. I got out of my bed and walked the room, but doing so just made me more tired and more anxious. If I thought about it too long, I got really weirded out by the idea I was being kept a prisoner by my friends. I didn't know what the taint would do to me, but I knew it would be bad. Really bad.

I decided that I had to plan for my death, even as I continued to embrace the faint hope of a cure. The Consortium would take care of Tamara financially, but she needed a parent. I knew Jessica would take Tamara as her own if I asked, but she already had Bryan, Jenny, and Rich Junior. He was just a toddler, and the son of Jess's husband and his mistress, both of whom were dead. Besides, I couldn't ignore the fact that with me gone, Tamara would have a chance to return to the real world and be, at least for her, a normal kid.

After Lorcan and Bert left for the evening, I used the house phone to buzz Jessica. Using it reminded me that I had never gotten my backpack or my cell phone. I wondered if Lor had found it or if he'd forgotten to even look for it. Oh, well. What did it matter now?

"Hey there!" Jessica said, her smile and her words *way* too cheery. "How are you feeling?"

"Like somebody hit me with a truck, backed over me, then did an Irish jig on me with spiked cleats."

Chuckling, she sat on the bed and held my hand. "What do you need? More pillows? More satellite channels? A bigger TV?"

"Five pillows are plenty and so are a thousand and three channels." I glanced at the flat-screen TV that took up nearly the whole wall in front of my bed. "I don't think you can get a bigger one in here."

"Point taken." She patted my hand and looked at me, a half smile on her lips. How many times had I sat on my mother's hospital bed doing the very same thing? I had felt helpless and afraid, though I never wanted Mom to know.

"In the library safe is a manila envelope. I need you to bring it to me, Jess, but please don't tell anyone else, okay?"

"Secret mommy stuff. Gotcha. Anything else?"

I nodded toward the mobile phone on the bedside table. "Can I call long distance on that?"

"You bet." Jessica stood up. "You want to let me in on what you're doing?"

"When the time is right." I smiled to deflect my reluctance to confide in her. "Ever figured out what the smell is up on the third floor?"

"Nope. I can't get anyone to go up there and check it out. The stench is worse than Bryan's room."

I laughed. "Now, that's *bad*."

When I awoke the following evening, I was greeted by the sight of Brigid bent over me. She smiled benevolently as she passed her hands above my body, uttering Gaelic in a lyrical voice.

I had seen Brigid in meetings and around Broken Heart. Yet I had never been this close to her. She was tall—at least six feet. Her hair was very long and red and her skin a creamy pale. She looked gorgeous in the simple green dress that adorned her. On her skin swirled gold patterns, as if they were animated tattoos. Jessica told me that Brigid was a true immortal, the mother to Ruadan and the grandmother to Patrick and Lorcan. She was also a healer with powerful *draíocht*, or magic. But she hadn't been able to interfere with the progression of the taint. Not even immortals had all the answers.

As her hands went over me once more, I felt a soothing heat flow from my feet to my head. The magic tingled and for once my weariness gave way to clarity.

"It seems you're preparing for a trip to the Other Side," she said in a lyrical Irish voice. "But maybe you shouldn't be packing your bags quite so soon."

"I'm trying to be realistic," I said.

"Is that your way of saying you're giving up?"

Anger spiked, even though Brigid's tone was kind. "I won't put my head in the sand and pretend that the taint isn't harming me."

Brigid waved at a cushioned chair and it glided across the carpeted floor. She sat down, her green eyes assessing me. "In the days when the Celts were one clan, when their magic hadn't been divided by those who loved the earth and those who loved the sea, I was born to Morrigu."

"Lorcan read me the story." I gulped. "The crow queen really is your mother?"

"That's always been the problem with mortals. They rely more on their eyes and their intelligence than they do their hearts and their intuition. Why do you think magic has faded so much from this world?"

"Lack of belief."

"And lack of practice." She smiled sadly. "The day I begged my mother to save Ruadan, grief knotted my soul and impaired my judgment. Maybe it would've been better to let him join his brothers on the Other Side. But I couldn't let him go."

"I'm sorry."

"There are rules, my darlin', for all of us. Even though I am as near to a goddess as you're likely to get, I can't just part the veil for a visit whenever I please. There is a balance we must maintain, no matter who we are or where we live. I need to focus on my work to be done in this world."

"Which doesn't include ridding vampires of the taint."

"Is there a reprimand in there?"

"I suppose there is."

"Do you believe there is a reason for livin'?"

"Is this a cog-in-the-clock-of-life lecture?" I chuckled. "I heard it from my mother and I've said it to my daughter."

"We are who we are for a grand reason. Not everyone knows their purpose, but they serve it all the same." She leaned forward and touched my shoulder. "You should tell him how you feel and ask him for what you want. Lorcan is a lovely soul, but as stubborn as—well, as you." She winked at me.

Then she faded away and it was as if she'd never been there.

I thought about what Brigid had said and shivered. If I was going to cross to the Other Side, I wanted only two things. One, that Tamara would be cared for and two, that I could make love to Lorcan. Making love to Lor seemed like a very selfish wish. I knew that he had feelings for me. And heavens above, the man could kiss.

Was it wrong to lust after a monk?

The phone call wasn't as heinous as I'd dreaded. A woman answered; her voice was cheerful as she called her husband to the phone.

"Evangeline?" Michael sounded both pleased and surprised.

Six months ago, I received a letter from Michael. It was the only secret I had ever kept from Tamara. My reasons for not responding to the letter were mixed, filled with right and wrong justifications. Michael had no parental rights. He'd made his position very clear sixteen years before. Tamara was mine and I couldn't bear the thought of sharing her. Then there was the fact that I was a vampire—how was I supposed to explain that? I sighed.

As much as I believed in the power of forgiveness, I had found precious little to give to Michael.

Now I had no choice. Tamara could live in a world where parents didn't drink blood for dinner.

"I'll be honest," I said. "I wasn't sure I would ever call you."

"I know you don't think I deserve a second chance."

Yes, you do. We all do.

"All I can say is that I was young and stupid. My parents—well, they made it easy to walk away from you, Eva."

I knew from Michael's letter that he was a very successful architect married to his college sweetheart. They had two children, a four-year-old boy and a ten-year-old girl. He had hired a private detective to find me, and once he had my address in Broken Heart, he'd mailed the letter. He wanted to see Tamara; he wanted to be part of her life. He offered to send child support, including back pay.

I wouldn't be human (figuratively) if I didn't admit to a little *nyah-nyah-nyah*ing. And, yes, I realized I had the upper hand. Michael would be my puppet and I would pull the strings. But these thoughts were unworthy and they didn't occupy my mind for too long. The truth was that I was scared. Scared of losing my daughter. I had been a single mother for too long. Like I said, I plain didn't want to share her.

"Evangeline?"

"I'm sorry." My throat knotted and my eyes ached with the need for tears. "I haven't talked to Tamara. I didn't tell her about your letter."

"I see." He paused.

"I'm dying, Michael. I need . . . would you . . . *shit*."

"How can I help? What do you need?"

"I need you to be her father. After I . . . when I . . . *go* . . . I need you to take her and raise her and *love* her." I cleared my throat, clutching the receiver so hard it cracked. "Are you willing to do that?"

"Yes." He didn't hesitate. I blessed him silently for making this difficult conversation easier on me. "When will you talk to her?"

"Soon. I didn't want to get her hopes up."

"I know this is difficult for you, Eva. But I want you to know how sorry I am about everything. I hope Tamara can forgive me. And I hope you can, too." He sighed and in that sound I heard his pain, his loss, his worry. Michael wasn't evil incarnate, not a two-dimensional creep. He was a man who'd made mistakes and choices, just like every other human being. At least he was trying to make things right. If he was reaching out his hand, then by golly, I would take it.

But I didn't know if Tamara would join the forgiveness train. As a teenager, she angsted about everything—from a pimple to a Cure song—but knowing that your father left you and your mother to fend for yourselves—yikes. Mending that wound would take a lot of work on Michael's part.

And I wouldn't be there to help.

"Evangeline?"

"I'm sorry. My mind keeps wandering. Let me talk to Tamara. I'll call you back." I hesitated. "What's your wife's name?"

"Susan."

"Is she . . . I mean, what's she like?"

"She's smart, kind, and funny. She reminds me of you."

It was the perfect thing to say. I pressed a hand against my aching, dry eyes.

"She's the one who said I should find you and Tamara and try to mend things. If you're worried about how she'll treat our daughter, believe me when I say she will love her."

Our daughter. Oh, my God. Never had a plural pronoun been applied to Tamara. I wasn't alone anymore. And neither was she.

"Thank you." I cleared my throat, but the knot tightening it wouldn't release. "I'll call you soon. Good-bye."

"Good-bye, Eva."

Lorcan came into my room and found me dry-crying. I heaved and whimpered, without shedding a tear, and I couldn't stop. He crawled into the bed with me and held me, cooing nonsense and stroking my hair.

I felt such pain—such horrible, wrenching pain—and I was drowning in it. The loose ends of my life were tying up. Tamara would have a father. The Consortium would have my library and my house. *And Lorcan* . . . I stopped blubbering and looked at him. He was the only loose end left, I supposed. How neatly the things in my life were weaving together—and it was a tapestry nearly finished. I should be grateful for such blessings. But fear blew through me like an Arctic wind. I didn't want to die.

Oh, God.

I cradled Lor's face between my hands and kissed him. When I pulled back, his silver eyes were mercurial. He took my hands and kissed each wrist. Pleasure zinged through me.

I gazed at him, words tumbling around in my mind. I wanted to tell him everything I felt, everything I wanted, but it wasn't fair. I would certainly feel better—the tapestry weaving its final threads—but I doubted Lorcan would appreciate my sentiments.

"If things were different," I said, "we could . . . date, I guess." I laughed at the idea of vampire dating. "I like being around you, talking to you, holding your hand. I wish we could—"

"Eva." He pressed a finger against my lips. Then he smiled—such a lovely smile he had and so rarely did he show it. My heart turned over in my chest. Oh, heavens, he was beautiful, right down to his soul. "There's something you should know, *a stóirín*."

"What?"

"I love you."

Chapter 21

"I love you, too." I hugged Lorcan tightly. Finally, someone loved me. I was worthy of love. Yes! All I'd ever, ever, *ever* wanted was someone to love me. *Oh, please . . . please love me.*

The Arctic wind blew again, chilling me to the bone. I shivered. Lorcan tucked me under the covers. "You are so lovely, Eva. It's too bad I had to give you the taint."

"But you . . . you didn't. You wouldn't."

"Yes, I did. And because I did, you must make me pay."

My teeth chattered. For a moment the room

blurred. Were there others around me? When did Jessica and Patrick and Stan get here? I heard snippets of voices.

What's wrong with her?

She's having a seizure. Hold her down. Where's the syringe?

What do you mean she's in the final stages? It's only been a couple of weeks.

Save her! Save her NOW!

Lorcan's roar made the whole room vibrate. "Lor?" I whispered.

I'm here, Eva. Don't go. Please don't go.

"Eva?" The beautiful voice drew me away from the chaos. I blinked and the people and the voices faded into nothing. I was in my room—no, my prison—with Lorcan.

"What's wrong?" I asked.

"Nothing's wrong, love. It's just you and me." He patted my clasped hands. His eyes glowed as bright as twinkling green stars. Oops. Wrong color. Silver. Lor's eyes were silver.

"I killed you," he said. "Then I gave you the taint. You should seek your revenge. You should kill me. An eye for an eye . . . a child for a child."

"Child for a . . . what are you talking about? What child?" I shook my head. "That doesn't make sense. I would never hurt you."

"No, you wouldn't. I keep forgetting that you're not bloodthirsty or vengeful. That presents quite the problem."

I felt dizzy, as if everything around me was falling away. My mind clouded, thickened with confusion. When it cleared again, I couldn't remember what had been said. What were we talking about? *I love you, Eva.* Excitement glimmered. Lorcan declared his love for me. Soothed by this memory, I smiled.

"Free me, Eva. Free me from the blackness of my soul."

"What? How?" My smile dimmed. "Forgive yourself, Lor. Didn't we already talk about this?"

"I can't forgive myself. I want to die. I want peace."

"No." Panic raced through me. What was he asking me to do? No, it wasn't fair. I was dying. I wouldn't leave Lorcan to the same fate.

"I love you. I love you so much." He sighed, his gaze sad. "If you love me, you'll do as I ask. I want to die. I want to be free."

A ribbon of understanding twirled. Oh, of course. That made sense. Lorcan wanted peace. I loved him enough to give him closure.

"I'll do as you ask," I said. "I'll do anything you ask."

"I know," he said softly. "Now sleep. When you wake up, we'll be together and you'll help me."

"Yes, Lorcan."

The prince kneeled by his dying soul mate and wiped the sweat from her brow. She was beautiful, even though her skin was as pale as the winter moon. Her eyes opened. As soon as she caught sight of his face, she smiled. "It's you," she said. "I knew you would come."

Overjoyed, he pressed a kiss to her forehead. "Yes, it is I. Your prince."

She chuckled, though the sound turned into a cough. "My prince of death. My angel of mercy. I am ready to go."

The prince's heart filled with dread. "No, my love. I am your soul mate. Worry not. I can give you life."

"I had a life," she said kindly. "It was a very good one. I was happy and blessed with friends and family."

"I've searched a thousand years for you." Desperation clawed at him. "And now that you are finally in my arms, I must let you go?"

"I am honored that you thought me worthy of such a sacrifice. Have your years been wasted, prince?"

"No. Never."

"I'm glad." She coughed and coughed. He wiped her mouth, terrified to see blood smeared on the cloth.

"I can save you."

"From what?" she asked, smiling. *"I don't fear death."*

For the first time in a long time the prince felt fear. He had the power to save his beloved—he need only force his blood into her and she would live forever. But that was his desire, not hers.

Love was not selfish.

Love was sacrifice.

—From *The Prince and the Maiden*,
an unpublished work by
Lorcan O'Halloran

"Eva?"

I awoke slowly. The room was dimly lit and felt cold. None of the electronics were on—no TV or CD player or reading lamps. It seemed weird, but it was almost as though I could feel the residual vibes of other people. But no one was in here now. No one but Lorcan.

I looked at him, at the man who loved me, and smiled. "Hello, there." My words sounded like a sexy purr. His gaze flashed with surprise, but I knew that he wanted me. And I wanted him.

He leaned forward and put his forehead against mine. "How do you feel?"

"Perfect now that you're here."

His lips brushed mine, then he scooted back. "We almost lost you."

"I'm not going anywhere. Not without you." I curled my finger in a beckoning signal. "C'mere."

Frowning, he lay next to me, propping his chin on his hand. "Are you sure you're okay? You don't quite seem like . . . you."

"I agreed to your request," I said. "Remember?"

"Request?"

"I will give you peace, Lorcan, just like you wanted. But first . . ." I kissed him. He fell onto the bed and I climbed on top of him, sliding along his muscled form. "You are so yummy."

"Eva, I don't think we should—"

I put my finger against his lips. "We won't bind. There's no need, is there? We'll give each other pleasure. I wouldn't feel right about keeping my promise if I didn't give you *this* at least."

I sat up, scooting so that the vee of my thighs cradled his hardening cock. I whipped off my nightgown.

"A stóirín," he murmured, his gaze feasting on my nakedness. "We must not do this."

"You want to," I said simply as I unbuttoned his shirt. The material parted. I bent down and kissed the revealed flesh. I felt extremely giddy.

Something's wrong. She's not like this. But . . . I can't stop. I don't want to stop.

I heard Lorcan's concerned thoughts and hesitated. What was I doing? Why was I lying on top of Lorcan? How had we ended up like this?

I want you, came the reassurance. *I want you and need you. I love you. Bring me peace, Eva. You promised. I cannot live without you. I cannot live. Remember?*

My purpose was renewed instantly. Of course! How could I have forgotten something so important? Lorcan needed me. He needed my love, yes, but more importantly, he needed me to end his suffering.

My worship of his body continued and like the beautiful Irish god he was, he accepted my homage. I kissed every inch of skin, flicking my tongue across his nipples. I teased them to hardness and bit lightly.

He groaned, and his hands dove into my hair and dragged me forward. His kiss was passionate . . . hot . . . consuming. I let him take my mouth again and again. I let the fires build and burn. Then I wrenched away and grasped at his pants. The zipper stuck in my trembling hands.

"Let me help," he said. The offending clothing sparkled away. Eager now, I gripped his hard length, stroking it with one hand, while with the other I cupped his balls and squeezed gently.

"I wish I could feel you inside me," I said as I crawled down and nestled between his legs. "But I'll settle for this . . ."

I licked his cock from base to tip. The musky scent of his maleness and the soft-hard feel of him against my lips delighted me. I stroked down until my mouth ghosted across his balls. I kissed them reverently. Then I pulled each one into the warm cave of my mouth, flicking and sucking lightly.

I released him from that sensual torture and attacked his cock again. I licked him, flattening my tongue against him as I sought his crown. When I reached the top, I sucked on the mushroomed head, flicking the sensitive ridge.

Once again, his hands dove into my hair and braced against my skull. He adjusted position, straining to get more deeply into my mouth. I accommodated him. I took every inch, slowly,

Michele Bardsley

teasing him as much as I could. I took him all, felt him brush the back of my throat.

Lust roared through me. It had been so long since I'd felt this way. I poured all my desire into this one act. I went down on him again and again, until he was thrusting and moaning. I maintained a thin edge of control—I had to, didn't I? Yes. I had to give him this last wonderful thing before I—

"Stop, love."

He rolled me onto my back and covered me, his cock nestled against my wet heat. His silver eyes were glazed with desire.

"I've never wanted anyone like I want you," he confessed.

"I feel the same about you," I said.

Smiling that wonderful smile, he dipped to taste my collarbone.

He didn't stop there.

Every touch made me shiver, made me want.

Lorcan stretched my arms above my head. My back arched slightly, pushing my aching breasts into his chest. My whole body was aflame. I wanted to extend this exquisite torture nearly as much as I wanted to feel the bright and shining end of it.

He kissed me, his tongue slipping into my

mouth to mimic the mating ritual we couldn't complete. I felt his cock jerk against my clit and I gasped.

Lorcan released my wrists so that he could cup my breasts. He pinched my nipples into hardness and I moaned as little shocks of need electrified me. When his mouth surrounded my nipple and his tongue flicked the peak, pleasure jolted through me, spearing me at the core. He laved my nipple, suckling it hard while his hand tormented the other breast. Then he switched mouth and hand and I almost died . . . again.

We were frenzied now, touching and kissing and groaning. I felt so savage, so edged with urgency that I could barely stand the overload of sensations. I wanted to scream.

Lorcan seemed to sense that I was more than ready. He pushed his cock between the slick folds of my labia and began to move.

Joy pierced me, trembling, aching tendrils that wrapped around me tighter and tighter.

"Lorcan," I whispered as my fingernails raked down his back. "Oh, Lorcan."

The orgasm swelled, waves of rapture threatening . . . then *wham!* I sailed over the threshold into bliss.

From far away, I heard Lorcan groan as he increased his pace. I couldn't believe it when my body revved for round two so quickly. The rocking of our bodies singed me to the core. The slap of flesh, the glazed look of lust in Lorcan's eyes, and his thick, pumping cock brought me to the brink again.

"Eva!"

His cock pulsed against my clit and the second orgasm bloomed as I felt the warmth of his come spray onto my belly.

He collapsed at my side, panting and sweating. He looked as though he'd been in battle rather than in bed. The thought made me giggle.

Whispering in Gaelic, he passed his hand over my spattered flesh and the area tingled. I looked down and found myself clean.

"I had no idea getting rid of the wet spot was another perk of being a vampire."

He grinned.

I flattened him to the bed and lay on top of him, enjoying the feel of being pressed against him. I rose up just enough to look him in the eye. "I'm ready to give you what you want. I promised."

His gaze shadowed. "What are you talking about, Eva? What promise?"

"The promise of peace."

"Oh, Eva . . ." I heard sorrow in his voice.

"Don't be sad." I licked his neck. The carotid artery . . . perfect. My fangs extended.

"Love, we need to talk. You should—"

Quick and deep. Hold on and no matter what I say, don't let go. Drain me. Kill me. End my suffering.

I lay my full weight on him, bracing my hands on either side of the bed.

Love overwhelmed me, guided me, and urged me onward.

If you love Lorcan, you will do this. Do it now.

I bit him.

Chapter 22

Blood gushed into my mouth. There was so much, it flowed between our bodies and onto the bed. It tasted wonderful. Powerful.

Lorcan yelled and cursed, struggling beneath me. I held on and I drank as much as I could, but most of it spattered on us. It smelled like rust, like death.

Close. So close.

I heard Lorcan muttering in Gaelic. Prayers. He was going to pass to the Other Side. Just like I would. We'd be together in heaven. We'd be forever happy.

Then my body lifted upward. I hurtled toward the ceiling but shuddered to a stop before slamming into it. Below me, the luscious, naked Lorcan was covered in blood. Without me to keep it open, the vicious wound on his neck began to heal.

"No!" I cried, flailing toward him. "No! I must end your pain!"

He rolled off the bed. With a few muttered words he was clean and dry and clothed. He stared at me as if I were a monster. As if I had betrayed him.

"Did you want revenge so much that you would seduce me and try to kill me? I believed you, Eva. I believed your words of forgiveness and of second chances. Did you think your final act on this earth would be to murder your murderer?"

"Why would I think that?" I asked, confused. I was trying to figure out why Lorcan was contradicting himself. If he wanted to die, then why didn't he let me finish the job? "You said if I loved you, I would end your suffering. You begged me to do it."

Realization dawned in his gaze. The fury sparkling in his silver eyes turned to horror. And I recognized pity, too. I had seen that emotion in a lot of eyes over the years. Everyone pitied me. They thought a young single mother without an education working as a waitress deserved pity. But I had been happy. My life had been good. Why pity me?

Slowly, I was lowered to the floor. Lorcan shot sparkles of gold at me. When I looked down, I too was clean, dry, and clothed. I was bound by a winding rope of gold light. Amazed, I stared at it. Why was Lorcan binding me? What was wrong?

"The taint has done this to you," he said. "I let my guilt and anger goad me into a reprehensible conclusion. We almost lost you last night. And tonight I had only hoped to speak with you, and I couldn't believe it when you . . . Oh, God. What have I done?"

When I awoke, my head hurt.

Ouch. I thought vampires couldn't get headaches.

The bed on which I slept was narrow and spongy-soft. After a few seconds, the throbbing in my skull relented and I sat up.

I wasn't in my fancy bedroom anymore.

I was in the prison. The *real* prison.

Terror assailed me. Why had they put me in *here*?

Scurrying off the bed, I paced the cell. I couldn't remember anything. Images were vague . . . fluttering away like fickle butterflies. I had gone to sleep the same as every night. And I had woken up here. I walked to the plastic barrier and pressed my palms against it. "Hello?"

No one answered.

I returned to the bed and sat down. I was wearing a pair of white silk pajamas. Lorcan's gold rose sparkled from its spot below my collarbone. My throat knotted. How could Jessica and Patrick lock me in here? How could Lorcan allow it?

Horror slowly infiltrated my fearful confusion.

I couldn't remember.

I vaguely recalled Lorcan coming into my room, but everything after that was a blank. I sure as hell didn't remember getting hauled into this place.

Had I done something terrible? Had the taint driven me mad? Then screwed with my memory? Or had someone else gotten inside my head?

These thoughts were beyond terrifying.

I sat on the cot and assessed the situation. I wasn't tired or confused or frustrated. Suddenly,

I realized I felt healthy and normal. But maybe that was the taint lying to me.

"Patient LeRoy, Evangeline L.," said an electronic voice. "Prepare for feeding."

I looked around the too-white room. It was big, square, boring, and sparse. Then I heard a whirring sound. A panel near the bed slid up and a small shelf popped out. On it was a plastic tube. I looked through the tiny square. I couldn't see anything; it was as if the tube was part of the wall. I picked it up. "What am I supposed to do with this?"

"Your donor is prepared. Insert the tube into your mouth, Patient LeRoy."

Temporarily resigned to my situation, I put the tube into my mouth. Blood shot through it. Human blood. Had they determined that donors weren't carriers of the taint? I thought about Bert. Where was he?

After a few moments, the blood stopped flowing. I put the tube onto the shelf. It retracted and the square door shut. I bet dollars to donuts I'd consumed a pint exactly.

"Hey!" I yelled. "Get someone in here. I want to know what's going on!"

Nobody responded. Frustration nipped at me.

"Where's my daughter? What have you done with Tamara?"

"Please remain calm, Patient LeRoy," said the electronic voice.

"Shut up," I muttered.

"Patient LeRoy is uncontrollable. Initiating measures to subdue."

"What?" I heard a hissing noise. I couldn't see the gas, but I could smell it. The air changed temperature as it filled the cell. "Stop!"

You would think that a vampire who didn't require breath wouldn't be affected by a gas, but with Dr. Stan Michaels on the job, chances were good that he'd figured out a way to do it. Drowsy, my vision blurring, I stumbled to the bed.

I couldn't believe this was happening to me. This was a bad dream. A nightmare. *Lorcan*, I sent out, *where are you?*

When I awoke from my forced nap, I thought immediately of Lorcan. *Are you there? Tell me if Tamara is all right.*

She is well.

Relief rolled through me. At least he could hear me. My heart clenched as I thought about my daughter. Did she know I was here?

She thinks you are undergoing treatments.

What did I do to deserve imprisonment? Did I hurt anybody? He didn't respond. Anxiety crawled into my gut. I stared out the clear plastic wall. The cell across from me was empty and the hallway was dimly lit. Seconds ticked by without a response.

Lorcan?

You don't remember?

I went to sleep in my bedroom and I woke up here. If something happened—oh, God. What did I do?

Nothing. You didn't hurt anybody. You were confused and a little . . . violent. We put you in the cell for your protection. I'm sorry, Eva, but I must go.

Wait! Where is everybody? I'm alone! Help me, Lorcan.

I am.

He left my mind and I knew instantly that no matter how many times I tried to connect with him, he wouldn't answer.

Scrabbling noises echoed down the hallway.

Faustus?

I could almost feel his pause. Then he said, *Who are you?*

It's me, Eva. I'm glad you are alive and well.

I am alive, at any rate.

The Consortium hadn't implemented their "kind" option of killing him. Or maybe the

Committee to Kill Prisoners hadn't convened yet. I wondered if I had made the list of consideration. The very idea that a group who knew nothing about me or what I wanted could decide to assassinate me made me feel helpless. And angry.

Is that you down the hall, Eva?

Yes. I woke up in this cell. I don't remember how I got here. I don't remember anything.

I can be of no help in that regard. Do you know what they plan for us?

No.

It does not matter. Death is what awaits me. The only question is by which method I will be dispatched.

Faustus . . . there is still hope.

He chuckled. *Do you know the story of Pandora's box?*

Of course. But the box was probably a jar. There is some confusion about the origins of the myth and even about Pandora—

Another chuckle caressed my mind. *The origin of the tale is unimportant, as are all of its incarnations. Scholars argue over the silliest things. So, to the point— When Pandora opened the box, all the evils were released into the world.*

And hope, too, I pointed out. *Hope helps us through the disappointments and the sorrows.*

Hope is evil, too. Hope gives us false beliefs. It allows us to distort reality and live in denial. Is it not better to face life squarely? To live with honor and to face the truth without flinching, no matter how painful . . . is that not better than hope?

I didn't want to concede his point, although it sounded uncomfortably close to my mother's philosophy. I believed my mother had decided she would rather pass from this life than fight an illness that had already won. After her death, I had devoured numerous books about every kind of spiritual philosophy and life-after-death theories. I remember one author saying that we all had exit points—that we decided when to die—we could stay or we could go. I wondered what the same author would think about vampires. Did near-immortals have exit points?

I turned my thoughts back to Faustus.

Why are you with the Wraiths?

I am no one's friend and no one's enemy. I felt his sigh ghost across my mind. *I contracted the taint. We were told that a lycan-blood transfusion was the first part of the cure. They blackmailed us into doing various tasks to get the second part.*

What was your task?

I was supposed to capture you, but both attempts failed. They promised me the final part of the cure if I would bring you to them.

I was surprised to know that he and the others had intentionally sought me out that first night. If I hadn't been looking for Lucky, would they have come to the house? Realization dawned. Oh, my God. Nefertiti had lured me to her location so that Faustus could take another go at me. She had known about my telepathic abilities. But how?

Why did you go with us? I asked.

Because you wanted me to go. I felt . . . compelled.

I glamoured you? I didn't mean to do that.

You would do well to learn your powers and harness them.

What's the point? I have the taint, too.

I am sorry. He hesitated. Then, *Do you have hope, Eva?*

Yes, I lied. *I always have hope.*

He was silent for so long, I thought he was done speaking to me. Then he said: *Eva, do you know where your daughter is?*

Chapter 23

Lorcan, why didn't you tell me Tamara is gone?
I didn't want to worry you. We are all search-ing for her, Eva. You have no need to worry.

You lied to me.

I am protecting you. Just as I intend to protect Tamara.

You are failing miserably!

Grief held me hostage. I would not lose my daughter. I was her mother. She was mine to protect, mine to care for, mine to rescue.

Damn it! Let me out!

I will contact you the minute we have her. I'm

sorry, Eva. It is in your best interest to stay in the facility.

He cut off contact. I wanted to scream. If my friends wouldn't help me, I had no choice.

Evangeline.

Lucifer sat on the end of the cot. Stunned, I stared at her. How the hell had she gotten in here? The cat watched me for a long moment, then tilted her head.

"Nefertiti," I whispered.

"Meow," she agreed. She leapt from the bed. I watched in amazement as she morphed into a petite, caramel-skinned beauty. Her long black hair fell to her waist. Except for the ankh necklace draped around her swanlike neck, she wore nothing.

I pointed at her, embarrassed. "Do you have to be naked?"

"You Americans," she said in a disgusted tone. Her voice was lovely, etched with an accent I couldn't place. "Such a distorted sense of modesty." She wandered around the cell. "Is this how your friends treat you? It appears you don't need enemies."

Too curious to stall the question, I asked,

"How could you Turn Johnny, then bind with him?"

"Because it was necessary." She laughed, but the sound was cruel. "I gave him immortality and power beyond imagining." She lifted an elegant shoulder. "I am royalty. He is nothing."

I wanted to tell her that she was selfish and unkind. Johnny deserved better than her. What would she do after the requisite hundred years were over? Probably find another victim.

"The taint worked much faster than we thought possible," she mused. "I hope you are able to serve your purpose before you die."

"Gee, thanks," I said. "But I called you, remember?"

"Did you?" she asked slyly. "They stuffed you into this cell and left you. That's so sad."

"I must've done something. They would never . . ." My tongue felt thick and unwieldy. I was suddenly glad I couldn't cry because I couldn't bear to show such weakness in front of this heartless woman. I thought getting the taint was bad enough. But losing my daughter and my friends and Lorcan, not to mention my freedom, was much worse.

Smirking, she sauntered toward me. She put

her palm on my forehead and looked deeply into my eyes. "You will accompany me."

The words flowed into my mind with cool arrogance. I envisioned each word as a soap bubble and popped every one. I pushed her arm off my head and said, "No."

She stared at me, her expression flabbergasted. "It should not be possible." Then her eyes narrowed. She leaned forward and touched the gold rose. "Lorcan's symbol. He protects you, but does not claim you." She pulled off the brooch and tossed it onto the bed. Cold rushed over me. The chill made me shiver inside and out.

Once again, Nefertiti put her palm on my forehead. I let her because I was curious about her so-called power. I prepared for her glamour, clearing my mind and erecting a psychic barrier.

"You will come with me," she uttered.

I looked into her dark eyes, assumed a zombie look, and said, "Nooooooooooo."

Rearing back as though I'd slapped her, she looked at me from head to toe. She didn't stay unsettled for long. Her expression turned calculating. "Do you know why Lorcan isn't here? Why everyone is gone?"

"I suppose you're going to tell me."

She smiled sweetly. "They are trying to rescue your precious Tamara."

Nefertiti was manipulative and untrustworthy, but in this case, I knew she was telling the truth. "You took her."

Sighing deeply, as though I had bored her beyond her capacity to tolerate, she sat on the cot and crossed her perfect legs. "The beasties have rebelled. We can no longer control them."

"So you need me to corral the mutants you created?" Zarking fardwarks. A werewolf round-up and me without my cowboy hat.

"A bargain, Eva. What you want in exchange for what I want." She lifted her slim hand and studied her nails. Her gaze flicked to mine. "I, too, once viewed the world as you do. Right and wrong. Good and evil. Cleopatra was my queen. The Romans won Egypt—and she died. They thought they owned us. They thought they could do anything they wanted." She sighed, a little too dramatically. "I was raped and killed by a Roman soldier. When I awoke, I was Turned and abandoned."

I felt a sliver of empathy for Nefertiti. I quickly squashed it. Feeling sorry for her would only lead me to assume she had the ability to feel sorry for others. Her humanity had been reshaped by her vampire experiences. Unlike Lorcan, Nefertiti didn't question the morality of her actions. She didn't care if she hurt others to reach her goals.

Lorcan, I sent out, *have you found Tamara?*

He didn't reply. Argh! I leaned my forehead against the wall and tried to decide what to do next. Other than Lorcan, the only people I could connect with weren't really people. Desperation raked me. *Damian, are you there?*

Nothing. Not even a whisper of thought from that guy.

My fears about Tamara's safety multiplied a hundredfold. I was her mother. I had relied too long on others to watch over her.

I had to use Nefertiti to get me out of this place and find out what was going on. My problem, of course, was that I carried the taint. For whatever reason, I felt good, but who knew how long that would last?

Indecisive, I paced the cell. Frustration roared through me. I had no one. Not one person to count on or to trust or to . . . help me.

"The enemy of my enemy is my friend," quoted Nefertiti.

"I don't trust you."

"That is your prerogative. But every moment

you waste debating right and wrong is a second on the clock of your daughter's life."

"You are such a bitch." It might not have been the most original description of a backstabbing, morally bankrupt woman, but it was all I could think of at the moment.

"Aw, now you've hurt my feelings."

"You don't have any feelings." I couldn't risk Tamara's safety, which meant I had to risk everyone else's. Once I made sure my daughter was unharmed and protected I would voluntarily return to my cell.

Nefertiti had managed to get inside a secured house, then into an even more secure lab without being noticed. Though she probably had the ability to sparkle in and out of places, she couldn't have gotten into the cells that way. During my first tour of the facility, Stan had explained that the cells were immune to that skill, mostly because of preventive spells cast by Lorcan and Patrick.

She toyed with the ankh necklace. "I will help you rescue your daughter."

That wasn't a good incentive for me. I didn't want Nefertiti anywhere near my child. All the same, I wouldn't be satisfied until I saw that Tamara was safe and sound. And I could use this opportunity to free Faustus. The man deserved to live—or to die as he wished.

"I want to take Faustus with us."

"Whatever." She rolled her eyes. "You'll have to get undressed. The spell doesn't work on clothes."

"What spell?"

Gripping the ankh, she whispered incomprehensibly. I expected her to turn into the cat, but instead her body turned translucent. She offered her hand. "You must hold on to me."

I found myself peeling off my pajamas. As vile as it was to touch Nefertiti, I grasped her hand. It felt squishy and cold. In an instant, my own body turned clear. I felt like a walking blob of Jell-O as we stepped through the cell door. Passing through a solid object hit number one on my Top Ten Weird Vampire Talents. It felt like being squeezed through a strainer.

When we arrived in the hallway, we solidified. Nefertiti let go of my hand.

"I need clothes," I said.

"Why?"

"Because I can't put on a cat suit and slink around like you do."

She led me to the entrance to the prison. On the left side of the door was a row of pegs. Each held a long white lab coat. I was getting seriously tired of the color white. "Beggars can't be choosers," I muttered as I took one and slipped it on. I buttoned it to my chin.

"You have two minutes to convince the lycan to come with us, Eva." Her eyes reminded me of obsidian. I think it riled her to know that she couldn't control me. "Do not betray me."

If I had been a tough heroine in a blockbuster movie, maybe Angelina Jolie in *Tomb Raider,* I might have snapped off "Or what?" But as Eva the animal-loving librarian, my response was . . . nothing.

The floor was as white and smooth as the walls. My bare feet slapped against the slick surface as I walked to the end of the hall to Faustus's cell.

Faustus waited for us. He gaze flicked to my ankles; he growled menacingly. I looked down and saw Nefertiti, now in the cat form of Lucifer, giving herself a bath. Yuck.

I don't like her, either. But she can free you.

Faustus raised his head to stare at me. *You cannot trust her. She never agrees to any pact unless she gains something from it.*

You wanted to get out, remember? She says that

your friends have rebelled and they've stolen my daughter.

She lies.

Does she lie about you?

His black lips pulled back and he bared his teeth. I was getting better at mind reading. I had seen an image flash into his mind, but that instant gave me all the information I needed.

Revenge is a terrible thing, isn't it? You killed her, so she Turned you.

Laughter filtered into my mind. *Ah, so she fed you that bullshit story about the Roman soldier who raped and killed her. I never raped her. I loved her.*

But you killed her?

Crime passionnel. *She was fucking half the Roman army. She made a fool of me! Nefertiti craves power and wealth, just like her bitch queen. At least Cleopatra did what she did for Egypt. There is honor in sacrifice for your people, for your country. Nefertiti serves only herself.*

His gaze once again flicked to Nefertiti. She had wandered away to look into the cell next to Faustus's. I had never known anyone as cold-hearted as she.

I will stay here, Eva. I would rather my enemy's sword pierce my heart than my friend's dagger stab me in the back.

I was disappointed by his decision, but it was his to make. *Take care, Faustus.*

Fac fortia et patere. He put his palm against the barrier. I put mine against it, too, and matched where his palm pressed. *Do brave deeds and endure.*

Chapter 24

I shed my clothing again so we could liquefy and go through the thick metal door that led out of the prison ward. I found another lab coat draped over a chair and slipped it on.

No one was in the laboratory, not even Stan, who practically lived down here. Uneasiness prickled my scalp. I followed Nefertiti up the stairs. The security door was wide open.

"Where is everyone?"

"Gone."

So Nefertiti wasn't so much clever as opportunistic. I *really* did not like her.

The house was dark and had the feel of hurried abandonment. In the foyer, I could see through to the formal living room. Furniture was knocked over, cushions ripped, glass shattered.

"What happened?"

"I told you," said Nefertiti. "The beasts rebelled. They attacked your friends and took your daughter."

Lorcan, Jessica, and everyone else must be dealing with the fallout. Had the mutant lycans or the Wraiths attacked? And was Tamara safe—or not?

"Take me to my daughter."

"Or you'll do what?" asked Nefertiti. "You're a *librarian*, for the love of Isis."

Her smirk grated on my last nerve. Before I could second-guess my actions, I grabbed her chin and stared into her soulless eyes. I seized her mind and demanded, "Take me to Tamara."

"Yes," said Nefertiti immediately. "I will do as you ask."

I released her chin. To make sure I was in control, I pointed to the curtains that framed the windows on either side of the front door. "Wrap one of those around yourself."

Nefertiti yanked off the pretty gold fabric and

created a toga for herself. She looked at me, her eyes glazed.

"Very good. Now take me to Tamara."

We left the house and walked down the curved driveway. The bushes that lined the drive shook, and then Bert bounded out of the shrubbery, barking joyously.

Nefertiti nearly shot out of her skin. She reared back and hissed. Bert paid no attention to her reaction. Instead he danced around me and barked some more.

Then he poked his cold, wet nose into my crotch. Oh, yuck. I gently pushed him away. "Whoa, there. I've told you this before, sweetheart. We're just friends."

He sat down and panted. I heard his thought: *Ham bone.*

"Later, Bert." I looked at Nefertiti and pointed to the Great Dane. It was wrong to give in to the childish urge, but I couldn't resist. "Pet the nice doggie."

She walked forward as if pulled by puppet strings. Her palm flattened stiffly against Bert's head. He growled and shook her off, backing out of her reach.

"You have good taste," I said to the dog. I looked at Nefertiti. "Let's go get Tamara."

We walked for a long time, down streets, through weed-choked yards, and around the broken and battered grounds of Putt 'Er There, the old mini-golf course. We didn't meet a single soul on our travels. Had everyone been drawn to the other side of town? I wondered what kind of catastrophe could rally every citizen. Then another thought struck: What if everyone had evacuated to the Consortium compound? What if they'd left me and Faustus to our fates? I couldn't believe that.

We followed the curve of a gravel road to a single, dilapidated house. It had been abandoned long before the vampires took over Broken Heart and started encouraging the humans to leave. Tucked into the embrace of tall trees and surrounded by scraggly hedges, it looked like the house that kids always dared each other to go into on Halloween night.

The flaking paint was so old that the color had faded to gray. Both of the front windows were broken and jagged glass glittered in the bright moonlight. The porch had collapsed and the front steps were missing, but that didn't stop Bert from leaping onto the rickety wood and sniffing around.

"Tamara is in there?"

Nefertiti nodded. I wondered if she was lying. Had she faked being glamoured by me to get me here? I looked at the creepy place, my nerves stringing tight. Why hadn't I thought about the possibility that Nefertiti might very well be leading me away from my daughter and into a trap? *Doofus giganticus.*

Bert started to bark furiously.

"Bert! Get down here!"

He obeyed me, skittering to a stop in front of me before wheeling around and engaging in another bark fest. The door swung inward and the shadowy form of a lycan hovered in the darkness of the house.

I'm Eva LeRoy. Where's my daughter?

The creature growled menacingly. Its snout emerged from the doorway, followed by its big, furry face. The rest of its body remained in shadow.

My heart leapt into my chest as fear pumped through me. I had no experience with kicking ass. If that thing attacked, Bert and I were lycan chow.

"Now, now. There's no reason to be rude." A tall, thin man emerged from the doorway. His legs were so long he crossed the porch in two strides and leapt over the broken stairs. His eyes sparkled. His brown hair was pulled back into a queue. He wore white from head to toe—a short-sleeved shirt, white dress pants, and shiny white shoes. His face was gaunt, his chin pointy. He looked like a too tall elf. Gold hoops, two each, sparkled from both ears. His thin lips were pulled into a smile, but it wasn't friendly. He looked at Bert for a second too long.

The Great Dane stopped barking and whined instead. He ducked his massive head and scurried behind me. His reaction freaked me out. Animals were very intuitive. If he felt scared of this man, I should probably be terrified.

"Where's my daughter?" I demanded. My experiences with Faustus and Nefertiti had taught me that I had power. A lot of power. I knew I had barely tapped into it, but I was willing to risk that my intuition was correct if it meant saving my daughter.

"She is alive and well." A Russian accent tinged his words. He looked at Nefertiti. "Though Nefertiti is an excellent prevaricator, she tries harder when she thinks she's double-crossing someone."

"She lied about the beasts kidnapping Tamara," I accused. "She would've brought me here no matter what."

Nefertiti sure was consistent in her evil. I wanted to make her go pet the nasty lycan staring at me from the busted doorway. I searched the house. The front windows were completely dark. Other than the lycan, there were no signs of life.

"I want to see Tamara."

"In due time." He studied me. "I didn't account for your abilities. Your powers are very strong." I half expected him to end the sentence with "young Jedi," because he was seriously putting on an Obi-Wan Kenobi act. Instead, I muttered, "Hooray for me."

His eyes flashed with humor. "It doesn't matter how you got here, only that you did." He looked at Nefertiti and shook his head. "She will not be happy to know that you are capable of controlling her." He snapped his fingers and Nefertiti blinked.

"What's going on?" she asked, plucking at the gold curtain. It didn't take her long to figure it out. "You!" She rounded on me, her eyes going flat with cold anger. "Never glamour me again, you Turn-blood bitch."

"Threaten me again," I said softly, "and I'll make sure you walk off a cliff." *A short one, so that the fall would only hurt her.* I didn't value her life all that much, but I liked Johnny and I didn't want to endanger him.

She lunged, hands aimed at my throat. The man grabbed her shoulder. "Calm yourself, Nefertiti. You have been bested. Deal with it."

Her hands flopped to her sides, but her fists clenched as if she might risk punching me. If looks could stake, I'd be one dead vampire.

"Return to your feline form and go to your post."

Nefertiti dropped her makeshift toga, grasped her ankh, and said the spell that turned her into Lucifer. She sauntered by me, tail whipping, and raked my ankle with her claws.

"Ow!" I tried to kick her, but she took off at a full run. I bent down to look at the wound. Red dotted my skin, but it was already healing from the strike. "She's meaner than Naomi Campbell."

He chuckled. "It seems your dog has abandoned you."

I looked over my shoulder and saw Bert loping away, toward the direction we'd walked from. I was glad he was getting out of danger, but I felt less brave without him.

"Shall we go inside?"

"I'd rather see my daughter." Fear that I had kept at bay now skittered up my spine.

"Let's have a chat first. You should probably know that I've launched a little attack on Broken Heart. Everyone will be quite busy for a while." He extended his arm in the direction of the house, as if he were a host instead of a lying kidnapper.

"You managed to regain control of your rebellion?" I asked. "Or there was no rebellion at all?"

"I have the same gifts you do, Eva. What do you think?"

The same gifts as me? I stared at the house. I did not want to go through that door. "I suppose I have no choice."

"That's not true. You can choose to walk with me into my humble abode or you can choose for me to carry you in there."

"I'll walk." I fell into step next to him. I couldn't begin to describe how nervous I felt. No, "nervous" wasn't the right word. I was scaling the heights to terror-stricken. "Do you have a name or should I just call you panjandrum?"

"That's very unkind," he responded. Humor laced his tone. "I am neither pompous nor pretentious. However, better a panjandrum, my dear, than a gobemouche like yourself."

"I am not gullible," I protested weakly. I couldn't help but be impressed with his knowledge of weird vocabulary. If he wasn't a bad guy, we might've had a grand time out-wording each other. He helped me over the stairs and the porch, then led me past the guard at the door. Whew. The beast smelled like rotting cabbage.

After creaking down the hallway with its cracked linoleum and peeling wallpaper, we entered a sumptuous room with bright colors and comfy furniture. It was luxury at its finest.

"You didn't answer my question," I said as we settled onto a fluffy blue couch. "Who are you?"

"Please forgive me," he said, his eyes glowing red for a split second. "My name is Koschei."

Chapter 25

"You're an Ancient? You're my—" Vampire father? Family chieftain? Evil leader? "Does the council know you're a bad guy?"

"Bad guy?" He laughed heartily. "The council rules its children, not its members. We make the laws. You follow them. Ah, Eva. You really are a gobemouche. Good and evil are a matter of perspective."

"I thought it more a matter of intent."

"Hmm. What shapes the intention of the act? A thief who steals bread to feed his hungry son is a good man doing a bad thing. A thief who steals bread to make a profit for himself is a bad man doing a bad thing." He waved his hand in dismissal and I saw the length of his fingernails. Who would keep their nails that shiny and sharp if not to use them as weapons?

I turned my attention back to the conversation. He hadn't gone through all the trouble to get me here just so we could have a discussion about ethics.

"So you believe it is not the act but the intention that determines what is good and what is evil?" he asked.

"I think good and evil are straightforward. And usually the people who tout shades-of-gray moral philosophy are trying to justify their own actions. Their *evil* actions."

"Or perhaps people who tout black-and-white moral philosophy have yet to commit an act that is considered evil but comes from good intent."

I sank lower into the couch. My lab coat felt very thin. One wrong cross of the legs and I would reveal just how naked I was under it. I felt vulnerable and uncertain. I couldn't quite believe I was sitting across from the creator of my Family. Had Koschei been a good man when

Ruadan Turned him? Had he turned evil—or had he hidden it?

"What do you want from me?" I asked. My voice trembled. I cleared my throat.

"Not what you think, lycan whisperer." He grinned at his joke. He tapped his long nail against his chin. "I find it fascinating that you experience telepathy with humans who can take animal forms, but my little experiments haven't rebelled. Another red herring, I'm afraid."

Stan had said the Wraiths were cloning blood and mutating it even more. I was reminded of Damian's story about rounding up his brethren to create a perfect army. Was Koschei trying to do the same thing with vampires?

"You've been cured of the taint, Eva—or haven't you noticed?"

I had noticed that I felt normal. The lethargy and confusion that had plagued me ceaselessly two days ago had disappeared. "Cured? That's impossible. There is no . . ." My voice trailed off. There was a cure. The one that had worked for Lorcan. Had I been transfused with royal lycan blood, too? You'd think that would be something I would remember—if not doing, at least agreeing to do.

Koschei's amber eyes snared mine. I couldn't

look away. I felt as though I was falling into that gaze until I was surrounded by jade, floating in it as though it were an ocean. I felt buoyed and safe.

"I command you to remember," said Koschei in a familiar voice that was so soothing, so compelling. "Remember all that you have done."

Memories flashed. *Lorcan loves me, begs for death.* The images flip forward. *Lorcan and I make love. I tear out his throat, drink his blood.*

Oh, my God.

"It's not true," I whispered. "I would never do that." But I knew that I had. No wonder Lorcan had imprisoned me. I had tried to kill him.

"Those who suffer from the taint lose their ability to differentiate between reality and fantasy. I found it easy to get inside your mind and make you see what I wanted." He grinned. "You've done an evil act, Eva. Oh, don't be so horrified. Think about how you have a comparison for our opposing viewpoints."

"I was coerced."

"Interesting, that. You coerced Nefertiti to get what you wanted."

I resisted the urge to defend myself. I wasn't a bad person. I did what I had to do. He was confusing the issue, trying to make me think I was like him.

"Why would you want me to hurt Lorcan?"

"I didn't want you to hurt him. I wanted you to rip out his throat." He leaned back and crossed his legs. "But something interesting happened. His blood cured you of the taint."

Hope wound through me. Did Lorcan hold the key to a real cure? Koschei could say whatever he liked. I wouldn't believe I was healthy until Stan himself gave me the news. Just like I wouldn't believe Tamara was okay until I saw her with my own two eyes.

"Lorcan's holding the key for the taint would've been a problem if not for you. Now I can kill him and keep you."

Koschei was not just evil—he was insane.

"You can't be sure my blood will cure the taint. Lorcan may be the direct source."

"We can do tests on him while we torture him to death. Two birds with one stone."

My terror was overwhelming. I didn't trust that my thoughts were my own. Koschei was powerful; he might be able to monitor my attempts to connect to Damian. I wouldn't call Lorcan—he would try to rescue me and be killed for his efforts.

"Of course, we will do the necessary tests on you first." He rose suddenly and held out his hand to me. "Come, Eva."

I didn't want to get up. I didn't want to obey him. But I found myself rising and taking his hand. My entire body tingled, then *pop!* We were standing in a dimly lit and dank basement. I could sense that there were things in the room—boxes stacked against walls, tables just outside the rim of light from the single bulb. We walked through this part to another section, which was brightly lit.

A man was chained to the wall. He looked like roadkill and smelled worse. His hair was stringy and oily, and he wore nothing but a pair of black boxers. The moment he saw Koschei, his eyes went red and his fangs emerged. He screamed and struggled, but his words were incomprehensible.

"Let me introduce you to Ron. He was the leader of the Wraiths. Now he's just a pathetic vampire dying from the taint." Koschei waved at Ron as if he was merely the busboy and the basement was a country club. "By the way, he's the one who infected you."

My stomach jumped in revulsion. Oh, God. This poor soul had bitten me? For the first time, anger flared, burning away some of my fear. "Why did you give me the taint?"

"Haven't we established I want to kill Lorcan? And I couldn't get to him, so I figured I'd kill some of his happiness first."

"Two birds, one stone," I muttered. "I get it." Giving me the taint was a backup. If I failed to murder Lorcan, I would still reinfect him. Instead, Lorcan's blood had healed me.

We continued walking, but I was reluctant to delve farther into the dank space. It smelled terrible and felt oppressive. I prayed that my daughter was not being kept in this place. Where was she? She must be so scared.

"Master?"

"Oh, look," said Koschei. "It's my newest walking refreshment stand."

We turned to face the man who'd called to Koschei. I nearly retched. "Charlie?"

My former donor looked awful. His clothes were stained and torn, his hair was dirty, and one lens of his glasses was cracked. But his color worried me the most. His skin was grayish white; he looked like a walking corpse. Even though he was the reason I had been drugged and given the taint, he had been my friend. I didn't want him to suffer.

"What did you do to him?"

"I would think that after his terrible betrayal, you'd be grateful I'd punished him."

"You punish those who do your bidding?"

He shrugged. "I didn't glamour him. I told him that if he did as I asked, I would give him . . . you. And the fool believed me." His grin flashed. "In his greed to possess you, he put aside his principles. Isn't that evil?"

"Only if desperation is evil."

"You are so droll." Koschei grabbed Charlie by the shoulder and sank his fangs into Charlie's neck. My friend's eyes glazed over, his hands pushing ineffectively at the vampire. After he was done drinking, Koschei grinned at me again, his teeth red with Charlie's blood. "Would you like some?"

My gorge rose. "Leave him alone. Please."

"How prettily you beg. No. No. I have claimed Charlie. He is my donor, drone, and doormat. Aren't you, my boy?"

"Yes, Master."

His dull gaze swept over me without a flicker of recognition. Is this how his life had been for the last few weeks? I pressed my hand to my roiling stomach.

"The more blood you consume, the stronger

you are," said Koschei. "The Consortium doesn't reveal that tidbit to its Turn-bloods. No, they are all about humane eating habits and keeping their humans alive. I don't understand all the fuss. There are more than enough humans to feast on whenever we choose."

"You're despicable."

Koschei pulled a handkerchief from his shirt pocket and dabbed at his bloodied mouth. "I tire of your hypocrisy, Eva."

My body was incapable of showing physical signs of fear, but terror and horror bloomed fully. I wasn't an ass-kicker or a smart aleck. I wasn't pretty enough to enamor Koschei and I wasn't brave enough to run away. And even if I'd had the nerve, I would never leave Tamara.

Feeling sorry for all of us standing in Koschei's torture chamber, I watched Charlie shuffle away. My heart broke for him. Then my gaze drifted to Ron. He had expended his energy. He sagged against the wall, his eyes closed. Drool dripped off his chin.

"I was abandoned in a prison cell," I said. "Nobody knows I'm gone. And if they did, nobody cares."

"Pity Town ahead," droned Koschei. "Population: You."

Lord-a-mercy, he was nuts. He grasped my elbow and led me to a shiny metal table.

He patted the table and I shook my head.

"Sit down, Eva."

His tone was beautiful, persuasive. I hopped onto the table because I couldn't resist his command.

Another man came from the shadows. He was short and stooped, with balding gray hair and beady black eyes. Dressed in a coat similar to mine, he studied me as though I were cream and he the cat. Though he was old, he was a vampire; his fangs glinted as he smiled.

A square metal table filled with mundane supplies such as cotton swabs and surgical instruments such as scalpels sat on the right. He plucked four gloves from the box and put them on.

"Otto, this is Eva. It appears that her failure to murder Lorcan was not a complete loss. In her veins we will find the cure for the taint."

"Excellent," said Otto, his German accent thick. "I look forward to . . . examining her."

Chapter 26

Eva! Where the bloody hell are you?
I didn't answer Lorcan's sudden, urgent plea when it popped into my mind. Instead, I let Otto take the scalpel to my wrist. The blood welled and he swabbed it, then put the long cotton swab into a plastic vial. The cut stung, but it healed quickly.

He cut again, three quick strokes up my arm.

I cried out. The slicing of my skin hurt. I wasn't brave, not at all. I hated to be in pain. But I wouldn't betray Lorcan again. Not after what I'd done to him. How could he ever trust me again? How could I trust myself, knowing that I was that vulnerable? If I could be glamoured into hurting Lorcan once, then I could be again.

What's wrong? I can feel your pain.

I didn't respond. I wished he would go away.

My heart is within your heart. I will not give up on you. Do not give up on me, a stóirín.

Oh, no. Not the poet. I resisted his mental pleas. I wanted more than anything to be rescued. I refused to trade my life for his. But I would trade Lorcan for Tamara. Nothing was more important than my child, not even the man I loved.

Otto seemed to enjoy taking the scalpel to me, especially when doing so elicited a pained response. Yet I could see no purpose in his efforts. Finally, Koschei put a hand on the old man's arm. "You can play later, Otto. Once she serves her purpose, she's all yours."

Otto didn't seem particularly happy to have his fun cut short, but he took a syringe from the table and prepared it. Then he swabbed my neck with alcohol and jabbed the needle into my carotid artery. OUCH!

I'm sorry that I locked you up, Eva. After you drank my blood, we were afraid you would change into a hybrid. I didn't abandon you. I swear it.

I wanted to reassure him, but I suspected Koschei was monitoring my thoughts.

"Why do you want Lorcan to die?" I asked Koschei.

Otto took another jab at my neck, and I flinched.

Koschei's eyes didn't flicker. He neither enjoyed nor empathized with my pain. "He killed my daughter."

"Well, he killed me, too, and you don't see me seeking revenge."

He shrugged. "I have made many vampires, but of the children born to me, only one remained."

"Ina?"

"Ah. You read the old stories." He leaned a hip against the table and clasped his hands. "I managed to Turn her. I lost everyone dear to me, all but her. Vampires must maintain relationships to keep our humanity. We must exercise our emotions, if you will, or we turn *droch fola*. Lorcan killed that connection when he took Ina's life."

I had no idea what to make of Koschei's accusation. I was feeling dizzy, thanks to Otto's enthusiastic removal of my blood. The doctor yanked my hair. "Ow!"

"For tests," he said gleefully. Then he jerked out a few more strands. I denied him the pleasure of my discomfort, staying still and silent. He scowled and returned to his table of tortures.

Eva? Please, love, answer me!

Oh, God. He sounded so desperate, so concerned. Would just one quick thought matter? Koschei was watching me closely. Otto had apparently finished gathering samples from me and returned to the dark recesses from which he'd slithered.

"Why don't you answer him?" asked Koschei.

"Who?"

His lips tugged into an awful smile. "Talk to him, Eva."

The urge to mentally connect with Lorcan was too strong. I fought against the command, but it was a short-lived battle. Koschei had been practicing his skills for more than four millennia. But not even a vampire Ancient is a match for a worried mother. I made a concerted effort to rebuff his glamour. I built a psychic barrier and strengthened it with my love for Tamara and my determination to see her safe.

It worked.

"You are much too powerful for a Turn-blood. What else did Lorcan's blood do to you?" His brows dipped, his lips pinching shut in anger. "Do as I say, Eva, if you value the life of your daughter."

"Free her and you can have me *and* Lorcan."

"Agreed. Tell him to meet us, alone, at the abandoned mini-golf course."

"I want to see Tamara before I agree to anything."

He clamped my shoulder, hatred flaring in his gaze, and the familiar tingling pricked me. We appeared in the hallway. Koschei hustled me into the living room.

Nefertiti waited on the blue couch. She had a nasty black gun trained on my daughter's forehead.

"Oh, my God! Tamara, are you okay?"

"Yeah. I'm f-fine."

Oh, my poor baby. She was dressed in a neon pink stretch top, a pink and black skirt, striped hose, and black platform shoes. Her body said Goth-punk, but her face said scared-little-girl. Her makeup was smeared from crying; black streaked her still-wet cheeks.

I turned to Koschei. "You made my daughter cry."

"Tears mean nothing to me."

That was it . . . that was it . . . that was *fucking*

it! Nobody threatened my daughter. Not even the master of my Family. I wrenched out of his grasp. Staring into his eyes, I said, "Freeze."

The word boomed from my lips. He stilled completely. Only his eyes revealed the depth of his fury.

I turned to the bitch on the couch. "Nefertiti, you will obey me."

"Yes, Eva."

"Stay where you are and point the gun at Koschei." I wrapped the words in iron will.

She swung the gun in his direction.

"Tamara, come here."

Eyes wide, she scooted off the couch, rounding the back to avoid getting in front of the gun. She hurried to my side and clung to my arm. "Holy shit, Mom."

"That about sums it up."

Hey, door jockey, I mentally called, *get your furry butt in here.*

I heard him scrabbling down the hallway. He took one look at the situation, and lurched forward, snarling.

"Freeze!"

In midlurch, he fell forward, and stayed with legs and feet still curled as if in movement.

"Go outside, Tamara, and wait for me."

For once, I didn't have to ask her twice to do something. She ran out of the room. I heard the front door slam.

I looked at Nefertiti. "Shoot Koschei," I ordered. "And don't stop until you're out of bullets."

Chapter 27

A s Tamara and I took off across the grass, we heard the report of the bullets. I steered Tamara in the direction of the compound, which was the most secure place in Broken Heart.

"Did you kill him?" asked Tamara.

"No. Not even a full clip of bullets will take down an Ancient for very long. We just needed time to escape."

"You should've killed him."

"Nobody knows what would happen to a Family if its Ancient died. Our powers are traced directly to the founder. If I killed Koschei, I might kill all of us from the Romanov line."

"Good point." She looked behind her. "Let's run faster."

I couldn't agree more, so we picked up our pace.

Lorcan?

He didn't respond. Foreboding whipped through me. Had Koschei's minions gotten to him?

Damian?

Eva! Where are you?

Tamara and I are headed toward the compound. Koschei the Second kidnapped us. I made Nefertiti shoot him.

You . . . what?

The bullets will slow him down, not kill him. He said his mutants attacked the town.

Several locations were assaulted all at once. Everything's under control now.

Good. Get to the abandoned house north of Putt 'Er There and nab the rest of the bad guys.

Done.

Wait! Where's Lorcan?

He was attacked. Stan is tending to his wounds, but a day's rest will heal him fully. I could feel his pause. Then: *Bert mauled him. I'm sorry, Eva. We had to put the dog down.*

Bert hadn't abandoned me at the creepy house. Koschei had given him a mental command to find Lorcan and harm him. Poor, sweet Bert. And Lorcan—he must've been shocked when his friend turned on him. Just like I had. My heart squeezed. I wish I could shoot Koschei myself. I'd empty every round into his balls.

"Mom, I gotta rest." Tamara stumbled to a stop and bent at the knees, trying to catch her breath. I realized then how fast I must've been going.

"Sorry," I said. "I won't feel safe until we're in the compound."

"Me, too." She straightened and looked at me. "Mom, you totally rocked in there. Yelling 'Freeze' was kinda cheesy, though."

I grinned. "It worked, didn't it?"

I was so relieved that Tamara was safe that I wrapped my arms around her and gave her a hug. For once, she didn't grumble and grouse about getting mommy-smooshed. She returned the hug fully and we stood there for a long moment. My baby. My sweet, sweet baby.

"Uh, Mom? Can't . . . breathe."

"Oh, all right." I released her and stepped

back. A flash of movement caught my eye. I shoved Tamara out of the way and she flew sideways, skidding across the dry grass.

Nefertiti shoved a long blade into my abdomen, and I pushed her away. Blood gushed from my wound, but it started to seal almost immediately.

"What are we going to do?" I asked. "Hack at each other all night?"

"I'm going to cut off your head, you Turnblood bitch."

Her knife flashed again. I tried to rear out of the way, but the blade grazed my throat. "Stop, Nefertiti!" I added the boom to my voice, but the dagger kept its trajectory.

"Ugh!" Nefertiti lurched forward, her arms dropping.

I looked down and saw that Tamara had gotten behind the vampire and shoved two very short knives into Nefertiti's sides, just below the rib cage. To my pride and horror, my little girl twisted the knives viciously, then ripped them out.

Nefertiti screamed.

Tamara pierced Nefertiti's shoulders and did the same shove, twist, and yank motion. Oh, my

God! My daughter would need therapy after this . . . or maybe I would.

"Don't ever touch my mother again," she said. She thrust the little blades into Nefertiti's back, executed the same moves, then put her foot onto Nefertiti's buttocks and pushed. Writhing and moaning, the vampire remained facefirst on the ground.

"Durry showed me the moves," said Tamara. "It takes longer for the flesh to heal when it's twisted."

"Tamara!"

Speak of the devil. The shout came from Durriken.

Still in shock over my daughter's vampire-hunter technique, I turned to find Durriken and Johnny running toward us. I happily backed away while Durriken secured Nefertiti's arms.

"My glamour didn't work," I said.

"She was in bloodlust," answered Durriken as he clasped chains to her ankles, too. "Vampires have more strength and resistance when they're really pissed off."

Johnny stood nearby. I turned to look at him.

"All these years . . . and there she is," he whispered. His hair was matted, his clothes dirty, and his smile grim. He must've been searching for her nonstop for weeks. "Nefertiti."

Durriken jerked the woman to her feet.

"I was tracking Tamara when I found Johnny scouting the woods. Then I caught Nefertiti's scent," said Durriken.

"Good thing," I said, shuddering to think how Nefertiti might well have killed us both.

"*O zalzaro khal peski piri,*" said Durriken. "Acid corrodes its own container. She has no soul. Evil cannot abide a conscience." He tugged on the chains binding Nefertiti's delicate wrists. "Don't bother trying to break them. Brigid herself created the *drabas* for them."

Nefertiti wasn't struggling. She was staring at Johnny. "Oh, my husband," she cried. "I wanted only to protect you."

"Liar," said Johnny softly. He strode forward and grabbed a fistful of Nefertiti's silky locks. "You cursed me. I watched my pregnant fiancée marry someone else. Another man raised our daughter." He twisted the knot of hair tighter, but she didn't flinch. "I hate you."

"I gave you immortality." She smirked at him. "You will live forever because of me."

"You're wrong. I'm just a walking dead man."

Johnny's other hand rose and in a flash of silver, Nefertiti's head separated from her shoulders.

Durriken shouted as blood sprayed him. He let go of the body and it slumped to the ground.

"Johnny! No!" Grief seared me as Tamara sought my embrace, burying her head on my shoulder. She sobbed for both of us.

He tossed Nefertiti's head onto the ground, then turned to look at me. His lips curved into the famous half smile that had made him such a movie-star heartthrob half a century ago. "It's okay, Eva. I'm free."

Nefertiti's corpse exploded into dust. And before my eyes, Johnny crumbled into ash.

Durriken went to report to his father, taking with him the Brigid-spelled chains and Nefertiti's magic ankh.

Jessica met us at the compound and led us to a small bungalow near the library. The place was sparsely furnished and was the color I'd come to dread: white. Jessica had brought me some clothes.

"After we found your pajamas in the cell, I thought you were running around nekkid."

I took the jeans and halter top. "You thought I was running around as a wolf."

She grinned.

At the same time I was putting on my clothes (oh, the glorious feel of pants), Patrick, Damian, and a large security team were bursting into Koschei's hideout.

Only Ron and Charlie remained. I don't know what happened to them, only that the Consortium spirited them away to another location. Koschei and Otto the Onerous had disappeared. Otto hadn't had time to pack up his stuff, so the Consortium confiscated files, samples, and equipment. Chances were good that Koschei, not Ron, was behind the sudden and virulent taint that had spread among vampires.

The first victim had been his daughter, Ina.

"My name's Ruadan." The man sitting on the steps of my front porch looked every bit as gorgeous as his twin sons.

Holy freaking frijole! Not only was he the father of Patrick and Lorcan, he was also the first vampire ever to walk the earth. "Should I bow or something, Your Highness?"

"My sons are trying to do away with the formalities of the Ancients. I tend to agree with them on the idea of relaxing protocol. Just call me Ruadan, darlin'."

"Okay, Ruadan Darling."

He laughed heartily, then patted the spot next to him. I sat down, keeping a foot between us.

The animals gathered around me as usual, which amused Ruadan no end. I had been waiting for Lorcan, hoping that he would visit me. I wasn't sure I could work up the nerve to seek him out.

My house would soon be emptied of its books, furniture, and memories.

Stan had given me a clean bill of health and was studying my blood. I didn't understand the scientific explanations. Somehow the royal lycan blood had fused to Lorcan's cells, creating a hybrid blood that destroyed the taint. Stan decided to work on a formula that could be directly injected into a sufferer. Faustus agreed to be the guinea pig.

"You'll do, now, won't you, darlin'?"

"Do for what?"

"For my son. I'm sure you know him: tall, black hair, tormented soul?"

I couldn't help but smile. "That sounds about right."

"Do you know that you're meant for him and he for you?"

"Oh, no, you don't! Jessica told me about the

fede ring and the soul mate story. You manipulated your son and the fates of the McCree women. You can't say the same about me and Lor."

"Sure an' I do," he said cheerfully. "But I didn't have to write Lor's story. He wrote his own. You're meant for him, Eva LeRoy."

"He probably doesn't think so." I sighed. "Ruadan, what about Koschei? Having an Ancient perpetuating death and destruction on vampires is not a good thing."

"He is *droch fola*," he said, his Irish lilt filled with anger. "Have no worries, darlin'. We will handle that horse's arse just fine."

I couldn't help but laugh.

He looked at me. "Now, about you and my son . . ."

"Your son can't forgive himself," I said. "My mother said forgiving other people was less about giving them absolution and more about keeping your own soul from shriveling up."

"True enough." He smiled kindly. "Your mother sounds like a remarkable woman."

"She was. We lost her five years ago to cancer."

"I'm sorry she's no longer on this plane of existence," said Ruadan, his gaze compassionate. "But I'm sure she watches over you and Tamara every day."

I tried to swallow the sudden knot in my throat. I hadn't had enough time with my mother. As much as I appreciated her now, there were plenty of times I hadn't. We had our share of arguments. We were both mule-stubborn and to this day I wished I had hugged her more, told her I loved her more. Did telling my mother at the end of her life how much she meant to me make up for all those times when anger and annoyance ruled my words and actions?

Every day was an opportunity to express love and gratitude. I tried not to waste those opportunities. You never knew how long you had with someone, whether it was sharing a five-minute elevator ride with a stranger or living an ordinary life with an extraordinary mother.

And maybe that was finally the lesson I had come to learn with Lorcan. I loved him. And I couldn't waste another moment pretending that I didn't.

"Lorcan will be here soon," said Ruadan. He winked. "Welcome to the family, love."

Chapter 28

Not five minutes after Ruadan sparkled away, Lorcan arrived. He flew in from the direction of the compound.

I felt awkward and uncertain. We had been through so much together. He killed me and then I tried to kill him. It didn't seem like murder attempts were the way to bring two broken souls together. So, instead of talking about us, we talked about everything else.

"Koschei is a much bigger problem for the vampire population than the Wraiths are," said

Lorcan. "Koschei and Otto are the ones really responsible for the vampire plague."

"Why does he think you killed Ina?" I asked.

"She realized what her father was doing and came to me for help."

"And she would do that because . . ."

"Once, long ago, we were more than friends."

"You were bound?" I don't know why I was so shocked that Lorcan had had prior relationships. He always seemed so lonely and monk-ish.

"I may have been a *filí*," said Lorcan, "but that didn't require me to be celibate." He put his arm around me and I relaxed. The tension dissolved and I enjoyed the easy affection. "By the time Ina reached me, the disease was in its final stages. I cared for her, but it was too late to save her. One night, she attacked me."

"It seems you keep getting attacked by those who are supposed to love you."

"Yet I'm still here." He smiled. "I didn't kill her, Eva. She walked into the dawn."

"Sometimes grief changes you. It makes you better or worse. Maybe Koschei needed someone to blame for his loss. Maybe he was always a little crazy and losing Ina was what broke him."

"Maybe." He kissed me. "I have to go, love. We have another meeting with the board. We also have to make preparations for the Ancients."

"They're coming here?"

"Right now, it's the safest place to host a conference."

Between the increased patrols, über-magic spells, and full-time vigilance of Ruadan, Broken Heart probably was the safest possible place for any paranormal being.

"They'll discuss what to do about Koschei. No Ancient has ever gone *droch fola*, and no one knows what will happen to the Family line if an Ancient dies." He stood up and I stood with him.

He kissed me lightly, then rose into the air.

I wanted to shout: *That's it? Where's the romantic gesture? The claim of undying love? The marriage proposal?*

Instead, I watched him until he disappeared, feeling bereft.

The countdown to the demolition of my home ticked to zero.

That night, I sat down on the porch steps for

the last time and petted the squirrel that had scurried into my lap.

Tamara and I had tried to get back to the way things had been before, but we were both changed.

We held a small memorial service for Johnny Angelo, though he had no grave. Jessica had declared that the old movie theater on Main Street would be restored and renamed Johnny Angelo Theatre. She even planned a weeklong movie marathon featuring all of Johnny's films.

I looked over my shoulder at my empty, forlorn house. All the books were now installed in the Consortium library. Tamara and I had picked out a nice ranch-style house within the compound. Not only would it give us extra security, but it was also near the school.

The Consortium council wasn't convinced I would be a good teacher, but with Jessica and Lorcan advocating for me, I had been given temporary teacher status. School was starting late, the second week of October. The first of the month was only days away and I had a lot to do. I was really nervous, but excited, too. Mom always said that when God closed a door, he opened a window. I guess the library was my closed door and the school my open window.

Still, I was grappling with the idea that to-morrow evening the house would be torn down and a security tower built.

Tamara had stayed at our new house. She was painting the walls of her bedroom dark purple and mourning the loss of Durriken. He and his family had gone on another hunt, but he promised to return before Christmas. He also gifted her with a BlackBerry. The boy could slay vampires *and* text-message. Now that's talent.

I guess the reason I had returned was not only to say good-bye to the house and to this chapter of my life but to see if Lucky would show up.

I missed him and worried that he had gotten hurt or worse. But maybe he had moved on. What I really hoped was that he had found his mate and was out in some lovely forest making puppies with her.

The relationship between Lorcan and me remained affectionate, but he kept me at arm's length. At least that's the way I felt. I do not know why I was so scared to tell Lorcan the truth about my feelings. I didn't want to be rejected, but mostly I didn't want to hear him say that he didn't love me.

As I continued to wallow in angst, I heard a howl.

I plucked the squirrel from my lap and put him on the stair. He chittered at me, obviously chewing me out for displacing him.

The soulful noise came again and I hurried into the yard and looked at the woods. Lucky bounded out of them, running toward me with joyful abandon. He slowed considerably when he reached the yard and stopped a couple of feet away.

I'm glad you're here, I sent to him. *I missed you.*

He sat on his haunches and yipped.

Then he started to change. The fur seemed to suck into his skin. His snout shortened and his limbs lengthened.

Within moments I was looking at Lorcan.

Chapter 29

"Oh, my God." Shocked, I stared at him. "You're Lucky? You're a *lycan*?"

He uttered Gaelic and a pair of faded blue jeans and a gray T-shirt appeared on his body. I noticed the concession to color; he had been retiring his mourning look.

Lorcan stood up, his silver gaze on mine. "It is the last thing I needed to tell you." He stepped toward me, gauging my reaction, but honestly, I was too stunned to move. My gorgeous wolf was . . . Lorcan?

"It started a couple months ago. The first time,

the change just . . . happened. After that, I learned to control it. When I walked around in wolf form, I felt compelled to visit you. You emit this . . . pulse that attracts the animals." He looked at me, his emotions shining in his eyes. "You were so beautiful and so kind. I watched you, Eva. I watched you and I fell in love with you." He looked uncertain now. "I have never found anyone like you. I want to spend forever with you."

Had some part of me known that Lorcan was Lucky? I don't know. I only know no other man had ever meant as much to me as he did. "Will I turn into a wolf, too?"

He shook his head. "I don't know. Will it matter, Eva? Will this be the one thing that keeps us apart?"

Was this why he couldn't commit to me? I wanted to laugh, to shout, to cry. I crossed the space between us and went into his open arms. He leaned down to kiss me and the flame of desire licked through me.

"I love you, too," I said.

"I want to bind with you, Eva."

"Here? Now?"

"If you can accept all the things I have done,

if you can accept who I am, and still love me . . .
then, please, Eva. Marry me."

"Yes." I kissed him again. "Yes!"

"First, there is the Claiming." He put his hand
on my neck and said, "You are mine."

Heat flared on my skin. I put my hand on
Lorcan's neck and said, "You are mine."

When I drew my hand away, I saw my ruby
symbol fused to the middle of a rose.

"If Tamara accepts me as her"— he gulped —
"father, then I will claim her as well. But only if
she wants me."

"She will," I assured him. "She knows a good
man when she sees one."

He nodded. "Then there is the Word-giving."
He drew away from me slightly and stared into
my eyes. "Eva, I promise to honor you, cherish
you, and love you for all my days."

"Not just a hundred years?"

"A hundred years won't be long enough, *a
stóirín*."

Grinning like a fool, I said, "I promise to
honor you, cherish you, and love you for all my
days."

I felt something electric arc between us. The
magic of love was binding us together.

"Finally, there is the Mating." He scooped me

into his arms. "I know that there is one piece of furniture left in the house."

"That's true. The sleigh bed."

Lorcan took me into the house, carrying me all the way to the basement, where my luxurious bed with all its pillows and soft sheets waited. Rose petals were strewn on the floor and the bed. Red and pink fairy lights danced above the bed.

"When did you do this?" I asked. It was the most romantic gesture I'd ever seen.

Lorcan smiled as he put me on the bed. He cupped his hands and whispered in Gaelic. Then he opened one hand and showed me the gold ring. The rose in the middle had been carved from a ruby.

"Ruby was my mother's name," I said, as my eyes ached with the need for tears. "That's why it's my symbol."

He slipped the beautiful ring onto my finger. "I love you."

"I can see that." I took a giddy moment to look at the ring, then gestured at my clothes. "Get rid of the clothes so we can do Step Three."

"As my wife commands." Another Gaelic spell was uttered and suddenly we were naked.

We lay together on the bed.

Lorcan took my mouth in a gentle caress. My lips were pliant, willing, and he deepened the kiss, thrusting his tongue inside to mate with mine. His hand slipped through my hair. I reveled in each tender gesture, each slow sensation caused by his patient tending of me.

His lips moved down my throat, lingering at the base. He trailed a path to my breasts, raining tiny kisses over each of them, cupping them in his hands to bring them closer to his mouth. His warm lips closed over one erect nipple, and pleasure shot through me.

He cupped the breast, which was still throbbing from his attention, and gently twisted the nipple. I gasped at the pleasure-pain invoked. As he pinched the still-wet nipple with his thumb and forefinger, he wrapped his lips around the taut peak of the neglected breast and sucked hard, nipping the end with his teeth.

I pressed closer to him, suddenly ravenous, needy. My hands glided over his smooth chest. I felt the ridges of his stomach muscles, the firm skin of his thighs, and the roundness of his ass. One hand cupped his buttocks, the other touched his cock, pressed against my stomach. With one finger, I stroked it from base to tip. I encircled the head, then slid my hand down its firm length.

He suckled, licked, nipped. I touched, stroked, and squeezed.

Lorcan's hand coasted down my stomach and found the nest of curls at the apex of my thighs. He gently pinched my clit between his thumb and forefinger, released the tiny nub, and pinched again.

I moaned.

He laved my nipples and slipped two fingers inside me. I moved in rhythm with his strokes and pressed his head against my breast, wanting more from him. He bit my nipple and the rough edge of his teeth sent pleasure cresting through me.

"I want you inside me," I said.

He parted my thighs and entered me slowly. I wrapped my legs around his waist and drew him in deeper.

With one hand, he captured my wrists and raised my arms above my head. With the other, he steadied himself. His cock filled me, his motions slow, steady, and tender. Oh, so tender.

His mercurial gaze captured mine. "I love you."

"Then show me."

He increased his pace, his strokes deep and sure. Still he held my wrists. I bucked against him, my clit throbbing.

A moan escaped his lips and he bent to sink his fangs into my neck.

My body went from slow burn to explosion. I was awash in need, desire. A buzzing climbed my spine, then zipped down again, sensation after sensation vibrating from my core.

The orgasm burst inside me, so brilliant, so pure, I cried out, caught in the web of pleasure.

Lorcan's ragged cry of release echoed mine.

We collapsed against each other, and he drew my hand down. He kissed my palm. "Now that I have you as my wife and that we will be a family, do you know what I am?"

"Hmm. What?"

He grinned. "Lucky."

Epilogue

Honoring the maiden's wishes, the prince tended to her throughout the evening. As her breath shallowed and her eyes fluttered closed, his heart squeezed in grief.

"I will stay with you and await the dawn," he promised. How could he fear dying when he was with the other half of his soul? "What is life," he asked the maiden, "without love? I would rather have this one night with you than another thousand years."

A beautiful glow emanated from his lady. The heat and light were filled with such all-encompassing joy, he feared it not.

As the radiance subsided, he found the maiden awake. He helped her to sit up and she cupped his face. "I was cursed," she said. "I was told that only a man who walked the night and who swore his devotion to me could break it."

Overjoyed, the prince took the maiden into his arms. "You were worth the wait," he whispered.

"As were you," she whispered back.

And they lived happily ever after . . .

—From *The Prince and the Maiden*,
by Lorcan O'Halloran

Read more of Lorcan's work in
Forever Night: A Collection of Short Stories
Coming soon from Broken Heart Press

A LETTER FROM TAMARA

Dear Dad,
    Thanks for the iPod. I really needed a device that can hold ten million songs. I am so not turning down a new laptop, either. I guess I can wait for Christmas. Heh-heh.

I think it's great that Mom had a miracle recovery, too. It was cool of you to offer to take care of me. I don't want to make this a big deal, but my home is in Broken Heart with Mom and Lorcan. And, yeah, my new stepdad is nice.

We just got a Great Dane puppy that we named Bert Again (long story). He's a clumsy goofball, but he likes our cats and he plays with the squirrels. The squirrels don't like it that much, but Bert Again keeps trying to make friends.

Quit worrying about my boyfriend. You're worse than Mom! I guess you can meet him—but you totally have to chill out. Anyway, Durriken is traveling with his parents and there's no ETA on his return. Happy? (That's a joke.)

I hope you understand why I want to wait until next summer to visit you. I know you're sorry and all, and I'm glad you want a second chance. I figure we'll be okay, Dad. I just need some time to process everything and get used to how much my life is changed. Tell everyone I said hi. I'll talk to you soon.

> Love and all that junk,
> Tamara

EVA'S REVISED GLOSSARY

Gaelic Irish Words and Phrases

a ghrá mo chroi: love of my heart

a stóirín: my little darling

a thaisce: my dear/darling/treasure

bard: poet-Druid (see *filí*); storyteller and singer of Celtic tribes

céardsearc: first love/beloved one

damnú air: damn it

deamhan fola: blood devil

droch fola: bad or evil blood

druid: philosopher, teacher, and judge of Celtic tribes

Glossary

filí: (Old Irish) poet-Druid (see *bard*)

Go dtachta an diabhal thú: May the devil choke you. (Irish curse)

Is minic a bhris béal duine a shrón: Many a time a man's mouth broke his nose.

leamhán sléibhe: wych elm (the only species of elm native to Ireland)

mo chroi: my heart

Ná glac pioc comhairle gan comhairle ban: Never take advice without a woman's guidance.

Níl neart air: (lit. There is no power in it) There is no helping it.

ovate: healer-Druid; healer and seer of Celtic tribes

solas: light

sonuachar: soul mate

súmaire fola: bloodsucker

Tír na Marbh: Land of the Dead

Titim gan éirí ort: May you fall without rising. (Irish curse)

Glossary

Other Words, Terms, and Phrases

centurion/centurio: professional officer in the Roman army in charge of a century, or *centuria*, of men

century/centuria: group of sixty to one hundred sixty men in the Roman infantry, led by a centurion

draba: spell/charm

Durriken: Romany boy's name that means "he who forecasts"

gadjikane: Romany for "non-Gypsy"

Liebling: German for "darling"

muló: Romany for "living dead"

Nein und abermals nein: A thousand times, no

Roma: member of nomadic people originating in northern India; Gypsies considered as a group

Romany/Romani: the language of the Roma

strigoi mort: Romanian vampire

Vampire Terms

Ancient: Refers to one of the original seven

vampires. The very first vampire was Ruadan, who is the biological father of Patrick and Lorcan. Several centuries ago, Ruadan and his sons took on the last name O'Halloran, which means "stranger from overseas."

Banning: (see World Between Worlds) Any vampire can be sent into limbo, but the spell must be cast by an Ancient or, in a few cases, their offspring. A vampire cannot be released from banning until he or she feels true remorse for evil acts. This happens rarely, which means that banning is not done lightly.

Binding: When vampires have consummation sex, they're bound together for a hundred years. This was Ruadan the First's brilliant idea to keep vamps from sexual intercourse while blood-taking. No one has ever broken a binding.

Consortium: About five hundred years ago, Patrick and Lorcan created the Consortium to figure out ways that paranormal folks could make the world a better place for all beings. Many sudden leaps in human medicine and technology have come from the Consortium's work.

donors: mortals who serve as sustenance for vampires. The Consortium screens and hires humans to be food sources. Donors are paid well and given living quarters. Not all vampires follow the guidelines created by the Consortium for feeding. A mortal may have been a donor without ever realizing it.

drone: mortals who do the bidding of their vampire Masters. The most famous was Igor—drone to Dracula. The Consortium's code of ethics forbids the use of drones, but plenty of vampires still use them.

Family: Every vampire can be traced to one of the seven Ancients. The Ancients are divided into the Seven Sacred Sects, also known as the Families.

gone to ground: When vampires secure places where they can lie undisturbed for centuries, they "go to ground." Usually they let someone know where they are located, but we don't know the resting locations of many vampires.

lycanthropes: also called lycans. These shapeshifters can shift from a human into a wolf. Lycans have been around for a long time and originated in Germany. They worship the lunar goddess, but they can change anytime they want. Their numbers are small because they don't have many females and most children born have only a fifty percent chance of living to the age of one.

Master: The vampire who successfully Turns a human is the new vamp's protector. Basically, a Master is supposed to show the Turn-blood how to survive as a vampire, unless another Master agrees to take over the education. A Turn-blood has the protection of the Family (see Family, Seven Sacred Sects) to which the Master belongs.

Roma: The Roma are cousins to full-blooded lycanthropes. They can change only on the night of the full moon. Just as full-blooded lycanthropes are raised to protect vampires, the Roma are raised to hunt vampires.

Seven Sacred Sects: The vampire tree has seven branches. Each branch is called a Family and each Family is directly traced to one of the seven Ancients. The older you are, the more mojo you get. A vampire's powers are related to the Family.

taint: The black plague for vampires. Thanks to experiments using Lorcan's unusual blood, Consortium scientists have formulated a cure for the disease.

Glossary

Turn-blood: A human who has been recently Turned into a vampire. If you're less than a century old, you're a Turn-blood.

Turning: Vampires can't have babies. They perpetuate the species by Turning humans. Unfortunately, only about one in ten humans Turned actually makes the transition.

World Between Worlds: The place between this plane and the next, where there is a void. Some people can slip back and forth between this "veil," but it's a sucky place to take a permanent vacation.

wraiths: Rogue vampires who believed they were the top of the food chain. It appears they have been disbanded and/or destroyed. Despite the best efforts of Consortium doctors, their leader, Ron aka Ragnvaldr, died from the taint.

Eva and Tamara's Word List

bugaboo: something that causes fear or worry; a make-believe monster

felicific: giving or getting intense pleasure

jollier: someone who jollies (banters, jokes)

minutiose: a person who concerns himself with minute details

Glossary

persifleur: one who banters, offers frivolous talk, and displays mild derisiveness

risibles: one's sense of humor; sense of the ridiculous

sarcast: one who uses sarcasm

splenetic: a sullen or bad-tempered person

subrisive: not quite laughing; smiling broadly

tramontane: barbarous

ustulation: the act of scorching or burning

wowser: a puritanical person

If you are a minutiose person or you enjoy erudition, Eva recommends the following books:

Ehrlich, Eugene. *The Highly Selective Thesaurus and Dictionary for the Extraordinarily Literate.* New York: HarperCollins, 1994, 1997.

Hook, J. N. *The Grand Panjandrum and 1,999 Other Rare, Useful, and Delightful Words and Expressions.* New York: Macmillan, 1980.

NOTE FROM THE AUTHOR

Death sucks. I don't know this from a personal perspective, unless we discuss the possibilities of reincarnation. No, my perspective is losing someone to the Great Beyond. My grandmother, Virginia LaVerna Smith, passed away during the writing of this book. She planned her funeral (she was very organized, a trait that has yet to manifest for me) and let me tell you, she knew a thing or three about dying (and not just because she took the journey herself). She lost her parents, two sisters and a brother, her three sons, and numerous friends. But she soldiered on, living life to the best of her ability, showering family and friends with love. She taught me to cook, she taught me to forgive, and she taught me the meaning of fortitude. In short, my grandmother freaking *rocked.*

If you still have the honor of grandparents in your life, pick up the phone, write a *real* letter, or go for a visit. Listen to their stories, hold their hands, kiss their cheeks, and enjoy their crankiness, their wisdom, and their memories.

Yeah, I got crazy with the Gaelic again. What can I say? I love me some Irish. I know I used "fola" and "fhola." I don't why I kept adding that *h* in there—it was probably spelled that way on a Web site, or maybe I secretly adore the letter *h.* Sorry. Also, I wrote "Lorcan" without any accent doodads like they appeared in the first book. It's the correct spelling, with or without accents, and let me tell you, the people in production have enough to deal with without adding an accented letter forty-one million times.

You'll notice I went crazy with vocabulary, too. Use my weirdness as an opportunity to annoy, amaze, or freakify your friends. If you know someone who whines, tell 'em, "Don't grex, you witling!" Translation: "Don't complain, you person with limited verbal grace." Heh.

Note from the Author

My research for this book went in several directions. I have a fondness for ancient cultures. You may notice how I crowbar in certain ideas (er . . . Faustus the Roman centurion) because that kind of stuff fascinates me. If it fascinates you, that's a sweet bonus.

In *I'm the Vampire, That's Why*, I created both a vampire and a Celtic mythos based on what I had read and researched. As I mentioned in my last author's note, a lot of ancient beliefs and folklore were oral traditions. As such, many weren't written down and we must rely on scholars and archaeologists to argue about which gods people worshiped four thousand years ago. Once again, we're dealing with cultures not known to have a written language. Slavic folklore and mythology are even more chaotic and disagreed-upon than ancient Celtic beliefs. Really. Go on and look up the *Book of Veles* for a large taste of what-the-hell. What I really appreciated about Slavic peoples was their *dvoeverie* (double faith). They embraced Christianity, but continued believing in their pagan gods—performing ancient rites right alongside attending Mass. Unfortunately the origins of many of these rituals and celebrations have been lost.

Note from the Author

What it all boils down to is this: I used what
I liked that was factual and whipped out my
creative license to mess with the rest. History,
schmistory. Any errors are mine and may have
been done on purpose . . . so there!

Here's an introduction from the heroine of the third book in the Broken Heart paranormal series by Michele Bardsley. . . .

BECAUSE YOUR VAMPIRE SAID SO

Hi, sweet stuff. My name's Patsy Donahue, and I'm an undead hairstylist. In Broken Heart, my clientele used to include housewives with bad roots, and strippers from the Barley & Boob Barn. Nowadays most of the females around these parts are vampires and really have no need for haircare. That leaves me with tending to those cutie-patootie lycanthropes and the occasional donor.

I have a son, Wilson, who is determined to drive me stark raving crazy, and doing a damned fine job. Then there are the ghosts. Oh, don't get me started on those interfering ol' hags. Can I help it that my family's power is necromancy? Talking to the spirits of the dead—could life get any weirder?

The answer is yes. Y'see, I sort of rescued this guy (hey, he rescued me first), and it turns out he's one of the most wanted werewolves on the planet. I spent eighteen years in a crappy marriage—I'm not about to spend even eighteen minutes with this silver-tongued devil who claims he's innocent.

But too bad for me. . . . He's so gorgeous. I've always had a helluva time staying away from those handsome bad-for-me men. . . .

My story comes out in June 2008, so look out for me . . . and hope for the best for my undead heart.

I'M THE VAMPIRE, THAT'S WHY

by Michele Bardsley

Does drinking blood make me a bad mother?

Broken Heart is the city with the highest rate of divorce and highest percentage of single parents in Oklahoma. And I, Jessica Matthews, have been a member of that club ever since my husband dumped me for his twentysomething secretary and then had the gall to die in a car accident.

Now I'm not just a single mother trying to make ends meet in this crazy world....I'm also a vampire. One minute I was taking out the garbage; the next I awoke sucking on the thigh of superhot vampire Patrick O'Halloran, who'd generously offered his femoral artery to save me.

But though my stretch marks have disappeared and my vision has improved, I can't rest until the thing that did this to me is caught. My kids' future is at stake... figuratively and literally. As is my sex life. Although I wouldn't mind finding myself attached to Patrick's juicy thigh again, I learned that once a vampire does the dirty deed, it hitches her to the object of her affection for at least one hundred years. I just don't know if I'm ready for that kind of commitment....

**Available wherever books are sold or at
penguin.com**